KOKODA MIST

KENNETH N. PRICE

Published in Australia by Sid Harta Books & Print Pty Ltd,
ABN: 34632585293
23 Stirling Crescent, Glen Waverley, Victoria 3150 Australia
Telephone: +61 3 9560 9920
E-mail: author@sidharta.com.au

First published in Australia 2023
This edition published 2023
Copyright © Kenneth N Price 2023
Cover design, typesetting: WorkingType (www.workingtype.com.au)

This book is a work of fiction. Any similarities to that of people
living or dead are purely coincidental.

Kenneth N Price
Kokoda Mist
ISBN: 978-1-922958-09-9
pp242

ABOUT THE AUTHOR

Kenneth Price is a Vietnam War veteran. When he was seventeen, he enlisted in the Australian Army and was trained as a medic. He was sent to Vietnam in 1968 and served with 8th Field Ambulance and 1st Australian Field Hospital. His grandfather served in the Royal Australian 9th Battalion in France from 1916 to 1918, and Kenneth's father served in the Australian Army during World War II. Kenneth's uncle also served as a bomber pilot in World War II and he was killed when his plane was shot down in 1944. After returning from Vietnam, Kenneth married and went to university where he graduated with an Arts degree (with Distinction), majoring in History and Literature. He also has a Bachelor of Education and a Masters (with Distinction) in Australian Political History.

Kenneth spent fourteen years teaching History and English at Brisbane Grammar School and eight years as a lecturer in English in Singapore, where he helped his students obtain their 'O' and 'A' level certificates from Cambridge University. Writing has always been his passion and following retirement he was inspired to research his family's military history. This led to writing his first book, *Broken Lives*, which covers some of the exploits of his grandfather's 9th Battalion, and now his second book, *Kokoda Mist*, covers his father and mother's generation. Kenneth has six children and eleven grandchildren. He is currently married to his second wife, Luz, and lives in Hervey Bay, Queensland.

BROKEN LIVES

Go into the trenches with the Australian troops of the 9th Battalion. Follow the exploits of Lieutenant Peter Bowen and Sergeant Craig Williams during the major battles of 1917 and 1918. Then go to the streets of Paris and London and observe 
the impact that the Great War had on the civilian population of these great cities. Follow Sister Ann Copley as she works selflessly to nurse the casualties of war. Observe some of the changes that took place at this time regarding the relationships between men and women, as they struggled to make sense of the upheaval to their society, which was happening all around them. Empathise with Yvette, a young 'war widow' whose life is turned upside down, and her struggle to find companionship and to forge a future for herself.

DEDICATION

This book is dedicated to
my mother and father:

Edna May Price
and Neville Kenworth Price.

T his is a photograph of my mother and father's wedding in 1947, just one week after my father returned from serving his country during World War II. Apparently, my grandfather asked my parents to wait for three months before getting married because theirs had been a wartime romance, and he wanted them to be certain about their love for each other. The next day, Mum and Dad went for walk. During the walk, Dad said, 'Why wait three months? Why not get married next month?' Mum agreed. They walked on; then Dad said, 'Why wait until next month? Why not get married in two weeks' time?' Again, Mum agreed. They walked on; then Dad said, 'Why wait two weeks. Why not get married next week?' Mum agreed and they were married just one week after

Dad returned from the war. They remained happily married for the rest of their long lives.

This is not a biography but a work of fiction; however, my mother and father were a source of inspiration for much of this story. My mother was a waitress in a café in Charters Towers during World War II, where she, and her fifteen-year-old sister, waited on many servicemen from America, Australia and New Zealand. The café was where she met my father. I drew heavily from her memory for the café scenes in this book.

My father was a soldier in the Australian Army during World War II. Originally, he was posted to an ambulance train that carried injured soldiers down the Queensland coast to the US Army 105th General Hospital located at Gatton in the Lockyer Valley. He then joined the 113th Australian Convalescent Depot and was posted to Morotai Island in the Indonesian Archipelago. After the war, he transferred to the British Commonwealth Occupation Force in Japan where he became a rail traffic officer (RTO) and was posted to Hiroshima Station. Yes, that Hiroshima, where the atomic bomb had been dropped.

I dedicate this book to my parents because I am proud of the service they gave to their country during World War II, and the contribution that their generation made in laying the foundation of our prosperous and free modern Australia. Theirs was a generation that spent their childhood trapped in their parents' hedonistic pursuits of the roaring 20s, their teenage years enduring the hardships of the 1930s Depression, and their young adulthood fighting to protect their country from invasion and the loss of its liberty. The rest of their lives was spent working long, hard hours to help build a nation with a strong, prosperous economy and a dedication to its liberty.

The values and principles that the fictional characters of Stan and Carol think about in the closing of this story are the ones my mother and father lived by. I think those values were shared by most Australians at that time. After all, theirs was the generation that produced the baby-boomer generation.

I am grateful to have had the parents I did, and thankful that their generation showed such confidence, courage and sacrifice to face almost overwhelming hardships and challenges during their lifetime. The majority of these Australians believed in a *fair go* for everybody, and the importance of good manners and common decency to ensure the continuance of a democratic civil society for their descendants – and a future my parents could only dream about.

PROLOGUE

On 7 December 1941, the Imperial Japanese Navy bombed Pearl Harbor, and crippled the American navy in the Pacific.

On 15 February 1942, the British military forces in Singapore, Britain's military stronghold in the Far-East, surrendered to the Imperial Japanese Army.

On 19 February 1942, the Imperial Japanese Navy carried out an aircraft-carrier-based attack on Darwin. It was the largest military attack ever fought on Australian soil.

These actions caused alarm among Australia's politicians and defence planners. Within the span of a few short months, everything they had depended on to protect Australia's security in the previous two decades had been brushed aside by the Japanese military like unwanted clutter.

On 21 February 1942, General Douglas MacArthur stood on the rear balcony of a railway carriage in Melbourne, Australia, and declared to the people of the Philippines, *I shall return.*

MacArthur had been ordered out of the Philippines, which was about to fall to the Imperial Japanese Army, and take up his new command as the supreme commander of the South-West Pacific in the allied war against the Imperial Japanese forces in the Pacific.

MacArthur delivered his speech to an awe-struck Australian audience of thousands, who had come to welcome the man who would save them from the terrifying thought of Japanese invasion and occupation. The Australians cheered, clapped and waved excitedly. What they did not know, however, was that all MacArthur had to offer them at that moment was himself and his headquarter staff sitting behind him in the railway carriage. The simple truth was that American support was months away, and all that MacArthur had at this vital moment in Australia's history was what the Australian military forces could offer him to command.

When MacArthur discovered just what he would be commanding, he was shocked. Most of Australia's regular fighting force were fighting overseas. The 8th Division, along with air force and naval personnel had been captured by the Japanese when Singapore fell. The 6th, 7th and 9th divisions, along with some naval ships and personnel, were fighting the Germans in North

Africa under the command of Lieutenant-General Sir Harold Alexander, who was Commander-in-Chief Middle East, and Winston Churchill, who headed the war cabinet in London and oversaw the defence of the British Empire. Churchill had ordered the Australian 6th Division to be part of a military force that had fought in the Greek campaign where it had sustained heavy losses and had to be rebuilt. The Greek campaign was badly planned and hastily executed (much like Churchill's Gallipoli campaign in World War I) and had failed in its mission to defend Greece.

These regular Australian troops had to be recalled by Australia's prime minister, John Curtin. What followed was a struggle between Winston Churchill, who wanted to keep the Australians in North Africa to defend the Empire, and Curtin, who wanted them brought back to defend the Australian homeland. Churchill believed that the primary mission of the Empire's forces was to stop the Germans in North Africa and the Japanese in Burma (now Myanmar), thereby denying them possession of the vital oil fields of the Middle East. Since Australia's defence ran counter to that mission, it could be sacrificed. Obviously, Curtin did not agree with this strategy, and ordered the Australian troops home to defend their homeland. Churchill resisted,

Curtin insisted, and so the Australians formed a convoy of ships led by the Royal Navy (RN) and set sail.

Unhappy with this turn of events, Churchill ordered the convoy to change direction when it was in the Indian Ocean and head for Burma. Curtin heard of this and demanded the return of Australia's troops. Churchill conceded.[1] In the final analysis, it would be the Americans, not the British, who would send their navy, army and air force to defend the Australian homeland in its 'darkest hour' of need. This led to a dramatic change in Australia's defence strategy, which would continue until the present day. This change is best summed up in Curtin's own words:

> The Australian Government, therefore, regards the Pacific struggle as [the] primary one in which the United States and Australia must have the fullest say in the direction of the democracies' fighting plan. Without any inhibitions of any kind, I make it quite clear that Australia looks to America, free of any pangs as to our traditional links of kinship with the United Kingdom.[2]

---

1   Lesley Carmen-Brown and Geraldine Ditchburn (eds). *John Curtin and International Relations During World War II*, John Curtin Ministerial Library, Perth, Western Australia, 1999.

2   *The Task Ahead* speech by Prime Minister John Curtin first published by The Herald (Melbourne), 27 December 1941.

At the time of General Douglas MacArthur's arrival in Australia, however, the only effective Australian fighting force available to him was a few CMF (citizen military force) divisions, which were comprised of part-time soldiers with only limited training. Furthermore, many of the units were not at full strength. Nevertheless, these were the soldiers who would be sent into battle in New Guinea to stem the Japanese advance until the regular Australian units could return and American troops could arrive to relieve them.

The call went out for more young men to join in the defence of their homeland, and young men stepped forward knowing that they would go into harm's way against a fighting force that had never been beaten in the field of battle and had a reputation for the brutal treatment of its prisoners. The Australian Government also introduced conscription for the first time in Australia's history to fill the depleted ranks of Australia's defence forces.

These young men were then sent into battle to fight in the New Guinea campaign and were ordered by their Australian leaders in Port Moresby to stand their ground against a well-trained, well-equipped, well-led and numerically superior Japanese force, while they themselves were poorly trained, poorly equipped, undermanned, and, with the exception of their field commanders, some of whom were World War I veterans, poorly led. These World War I veteran field commanders knew how to establish fields of fire and crossfire killing zones, so effective against an enemy determined to make repeated frontal assaults, which was the tactic that the Japanese commander, Lieutenant General Hatazo Adachi, adopted because he was working to a very short timetable to take Port Moresby. The Australian field commanders also reasoned that since they couldn't stop the Japanese advance, the best they could do was to slow it down, so they employed the tactic of a fighting withdrawal, allowing time for Port Moresby to be fortified and time for the regular Australian soldiers to return from North Africa, and American troops to arrive from America.

Their Australian headquarter leaders in Port Moresby, and their American counterparts in Brisbane, however, were making decisions based on faulty intelligence about the strength of the Japanese force they were fighting. They also had little appreciation of the terrain these young men were fighting in, and no regard for the inadequate supplies their soldiers were receiving. The soldiers they commanded had to fight with World War I weaponry, wear uniforms that had been designed for desert warfare that offered no camouflage protection and quickly deteriorated in the tropical climate, and contend with tropical diseases never experienced by Australian soldiers before. They were surviving on food supplies that were inappropriate, insufficient, and often spoiled by their exposure to the climate.

What these young men had, however, was an abundance of courage and a heroic fighting spirit that was undaunted and determined not to let the Japanese invade their homeland. And so it was that the soldiers of the Australian 39th Battalion found themselves trying to hold out against the onslaught of the infamous Japanese South Seas Detachment as wave after wave of fanatical Japanese warriors broke upon their ranks …

CHAPTER 1

They'll be here *any moment now,* Stan thought, looking up at the huge clouds threatening to break at any moment. The heat and humidity that had been building all day closed in around him. Sweat trickled down his chest and face, soaking his belly and neck. Without turning, he tightened his grip on his .303 rifle, and pulled it snugly into his shoulder.

When they came into view, he was surprised to see how tall they were. He was expecting to see five-foot men, but those who came into the straight stretch of track were six feet or more and they were wheeling pushbikes – useless on the Kokoda Track.

'Let the first ten or so pass before you open fire,' he had been told, and so he waited, nerves tingling throughout his body, for the right moment. *Just a few more, then we can have at 'em,* Stan thought, but the Australians opened fire before he had anticipated.

The battle exploded rapidly. Australian firepower, delivered by old World War I Lewis machine guns and .303 rifles, ripped through the jungle undergrowth.

Leaves fluttered and branches fell as the bullets tore through and smashed into the advance guard of Japanese soldiers.

Caught in the open, many Japanese fell. Stan picked his targets with ease, reloading manually, the bolt of his .303 sliding smoothly, ejecting spent cartridges and popping live ones into the firing chamber. He got off three shots before the stunned Japanese began to react. Some went to ground and returned fire, others retreated to re-group with their main body further down the track. The Japanese then fanned out on either side of the track and started a sweep through the jungle.

With the Japanese soldiers lying on the track, moaning and clutching their wounds or laying in silent death, Stan and the rest of his squad picked their way back through the jungle to regroup with their platoon.

After regrouping, the Australians spread themselves out across each side of the track, anticipating the Japanese onslaught. They did not have long to wait. Amid screams of *Banzai!* the Japanese launched themselves at the Australians, whose firepower managed to hold them off, but the Australians were heavily outnumbered. They knew it would only be a matter of time before the Japanese found the outer limits of their flanks and moved around to surround them. The Australian commander was worried that his men would be cut off, and that new arrivals, coming down the track from Kokoda, would walk into an ambush. Before anything could be done, however, the Japanese encirclement was complete.

The Australians had waited too long before withdrawing back to Kokoda. They had intended to slow the Japanese advance by fighting with hit-and-run tactics before making a stand with their full strength. Now it appeared too late. The small band of Australians would have to fight their way out against unbeatable odds.

Stan kept reloading and firing; his targets were not hard to find, they were only a few yards in front of him, and even though his hands began to shake, he kept on firing until his magazine emptied. Bravely, the Australian commander rose and attempted to contact the Australian reinforcements. He was killed instantly. At this point, Stan felt a panic rise within him. Knowing how much his mates depended on him to keep fighting, he smothered the instinct to cut and run.

Just then, an image of Carol came into his mind. He saw her cradling her newborn sister, Jean, in her arms. Carol smiled as she sat, gently caressing her sister's head.

'You're my little girl now,' she had whispered.

Carol and Stan had grown up together back in Brisbane. They were close friends who shared the hardship of having lost a parent. Carol's mother had died giving birth to Jean, while Stan's father had died in an accident at work. Carol's father worked on the docks in Brisbane which kept him away from home for long hours. Stan and his mother survived on the insurance money his mother got after his father's death and what she earned from cleaning offices at night. Having to take on responsibilities beyond their years had brought Stan and Carol together in a special way.

Instantly, a calmness fell upon him. He regained control and changed the empty magazine with a full one; then, he continued firing with renewed determination.

If I die now, Carol, I'll take a few of these bastards with me, he promised her.

The Lewis gun beside him kept hammering away at the charging Japanese, who kept falling away before them. Segments of the Australian line were separated in the confusion of battle as the Japanese penetrated their line of defence, but the Australian centre, where Stan was, continued to hold.

With one final, determined rush, the Japanese launched themselves at the Australian centre.

Hand-to-hand fighting erupted around Stan. The din of battle echoed in his ears. Grunts, groans and the thudding of blows mixed with shouting and screaming echoed in his ears. He used the butt of his rifle like a club, smashing anything he saw in front of him. Suddenly, a sharp pain exploded in the back of his head. Darkness engulfed him as he fell forward and rolled over in the soft, damp leaves lining the Kokoda Track.

*

Carol Sutton stopped to look back and smiled brightly at the child-like antics of her younger sister, Jean, whose face was locked in concentration as she carefully placed her foot on the concrete strip atop the gutter she was balancing on. Her arms were extended, giving balance to her slender, young body. Gradually she increased her pace, her confidence growing with each step.

Jean craves adventure, Carol thought, *although Father would probably say Jean was more rebellious than adventurous.*

The two of them were always clashing over Jean's behaviour. Sometimes their father was right, sometimes he went too far, but whatever he said, Jean was developing the habit of defying him, leaving Carol in the middle – caught between the two people she loved most in this world.

Jean was an attractive, shapely, sixteen-year-old teenage girl. She had blond hair, bright blue eyes and white teeth that flashed whenever she smiled, which was often. Carol, on the other hand, was a brunette with large brown eyes and generous red lips. When she smiled her whole face lit up, especially her eyes. She was also attractive, but in a more homely, wholesome way.

Looking at Jean, Carol's heart filled. They had been so close from the first day of Jean's life, sixteen years ago. Jean was born at home, and Carol, barely five at the time, was allowed to see her newborn sister late in the afternoon. She had stood next to an old cot given to her mother by a thoughtful neighbour. Carol remembered how delighted she had been to see her sister, and how distressed she was over her mother's death.

Conflicting emotions had battled for her attention on that day, while concern for her family's future had heightened her anxiety. Through it all, however, one thing had become clear to her – she had to protect her sister, who was so small, and so perfect. When Jean had opened her eyes, the blue intensity of her unfocused gaze seemed to reach a point deep inside Carol.

You are so beautiful, I wish you were mine, she had thought then, and that feeling had not diminished.

Carol's motherly instinct had intensified after Jean came to her for advice when she got her first period. Poor young Jean was so concerned and earnest about what was happening to her, but after Carol explained that it was natural for all mature women to go through a monthly cycle so they could have children, Jean had become more accepting of her womanly fate. Jean had already developed a mature, curvaceous body, and needed Carol's advice and guidance more than ever.

Carol checked the time on her watch, and realised they were running behind schedule. 'We'll have to hurry if we're going to make work on time, Jean.'

'There's plenty of time,' Jean replied, looking up. 'Why do you always worry … Shit! Carol!' Jean shouted, losing her footing and pitching forward. Carol rushed forward and caught her sister just before she fell.

'Nearly pissed myself,' Jean giggled.

'Watch what you say in public,' Carol protested, averting her eyes from a glaring matron standing nearby. They locked arms and bounced towards the Victory Café where they both worked as waitresses.

With smiling faces, the girls bounded through the open doorway of the café, flanked on either side with huge bay windows. One window proclaimed in bold letters, VICTORY CAFÉ, while the other proudly displayed American and Australian flags with poles crossed. Beryl Cooper was the café owner, and this was her way of trying to bring peace, or at least tolerance, between the American and Australian troops who frequented her establishment. The Americans were primarily support staff for the American headquarters now located in Brisbane and comprised mainly of air force personnel and engineers who were building infrastructure necessary for the troops. Warehouses, concrete roads and camps seemed to spring up overnight everywhere. However, the bulk of their fighting force was still some time away.

'Save it for the Japs, or take it outside!' Beryl would shout at any troublemakers who looked like they were about to start a fight. 'If you boys could just get along with each other, there isn't an army in the world that could stand up to you,' she would add as a consoling thought to flared tempers.

'Morning, Mrs Cooper,' Carol and Jean said in unison, smiling at Beryl as they entered.

'Morning, girls. As you can see, we're busy again, but keep those beaming smiles for the customers.'

'We'll start right away, Mrs Cooper,' Carol chirped.

As the girls moved off, Jean's footing suddenly slipped. She reached for Carol's arm. 'Oops!' Jean grunted.

'You seem to have the slipsies this morning,' Carol said, holding onto Jean's arm.

'Yeah, it's these new shoes. I'll have to replace the leather soles.'

A look of concern crossed Beryl's face. 'We just had the floors polished last night and it's still slippery. You'll have to be careful, Jean.'

'Yes, Mrs Cooper.' Jean smiled and, with exaggerated steps, tiptoed to the kitchen.

For Carol, working at the Victory Café was a godsend. Before the war, and before the Americans arrived, Carol had worked as a domestic for the headmaster of a local school and his family. Her hours were from 7 am until 7 pm, including Saturdays. She worked hard: cooking, cleaning, sewing, and taking care of the children. The headmaster's wife was no help, always having something to do downtown or retiring to her bedroom to read or to nurse a migraine. Carol often found herself in tears but managed to keep them to herself. For all that, Carol was paid a meagre ten shillings per week, money that was desperately needed by her family.

Since joining Mrs Cooper's staff, however, Carol worked shifts. The morning shift was from 6 am to

2 pm, the evening shift from 2 pm to 10 pm, and the night shift from 10 pm to 6 am. The morning shift was the busiest, taking in both breakfast and lunch, but no one minded because everyone took turns, so there was no favouritism. For this work, Carol was paid thirty shillings per week, which was a godsend for her and her family. Beryl was there the whole time, by the cash register. From there, she could see who came in and out, and she could take personal charge of the money and *her girls* as they moved around the tables taking orders from the customers, mainly young soldiers – Americans, Australians and some New Zealanders. Occasionally, Beryl would retire to a back room where she took naps in a specially prepared bed.

Pressing down her apron, Carol entered from the back. She stopped at a table seating four American GIs. 'What are you boys having?' she asked, taking an order book from her apron pocket and a pencil from behind her ear.

The GI nearest her put his hand up to his chin and smiled, 'Why, honey, I thought I might start with you,' he teased.

Carol frowned. 'Do you get very far with that line?' she scowled.

Beryl looked up as the other GIs laughed. 'Guess ya goin' home alone tonight, young man,' she called out.

The American laughed. 'Reckon yer right at that.'

Carol took their orders, then went out back to tell the cook what was wanted. The Americans settled back into their light-hearted banter.

When Carol had asked Beryl whether Jean could work as a waitress, she had immediately agreed. The fact that Jean was only sixteen years old had made little impact on Beryl. With the wartime shortage of labour, all the café owners were employing younger waitresses. Some as young as thirteen. Sixteen, however, was the youngest that Beryl would have in her establishment.

Jean, who had started working right away, was an instant success with the Americans. They began returning and would always look for her to serve them. 'Hey. Where's my angel?' they would ask.

'Which angel did you have in mind, honey?' Beryl would tease.

'You know there's only one for me. Jean. The one with the angel face.'

There was something in Jean's smile and her eyes that seemed to promise more than just a meal. Also, she had a freshness, an innocence that reminded soldiers of home and happier times. They flirted with Jean a lot, but it was nothing more than that, just flirting.

One time, Jean's father came to the café. 'Hello Mrs Cooper. I'm Jean's father, Alan Sutton.'

Beryl stared at him, waiting for him to continue.

'Uh … well, I was wondering if you could keep an eye on Jean for me. She being so young … with the soldiers and all … I'm worried,' he said.

Beryl took her time answering. 'Look Mr Sutton, I like Jean, and, of course, I look out for her here at work, but when she leaves work, I can't be held responsible. What happens after she walks through that door after work is her business. And yours. Not mine.'

Alan's eyes dropped. It seemed like he was going to say something but didn't. Finally, as he looked up, he replied, 'Yes. Well, I guess that's the way of it then.'

*

The late-afternoon rush was on in earnest. The waitresses, taking orders and delivering plates of mainly steak and eggs, rushed in and out of the kitchen and eating areas. A soldier's hunger was usually satisfied with simple but substantial food, offering a break from the blandness of rations or reheated meals from their unit kitchens.

Carrying three plates of food, Jean burst through the swinging out doors of the kitchen and hurried to the front of the café. Suddenly, her feet went from under her. She fell on her backside and began to slide down the passage, bravely balancing the plates of food. The whole café went quiet as everyone watched her. Even Beryl stopped taking money from a customer to watch. The expected calamity of Jean and food ending in a soggy mess did not materialise, however. Instead, she managed to hold it all together until her short slide left her between two American signal sergeants, who stood talking in the passage.

She looked up into the eyes of a clean, handsome face. There was a long pause before the young American soldier said, 'Hello, Angel. Which heaven did you just fall from?'

Keeping her eyes locked with his, she could only smile back as the café erupted into laughter and applause.

'Here, honey. Let me help you up,' the young soldier said. He stepped behind her, reached down and placed his hands under her armpits, then raised her to her feet.

'Thank you,' Jean whispered, lowering her gaze.

Suddenly, Beryl was beside her. 'Are you all right, Jean?' she asked.

Jean turned to face her. 'Yes. I'm fine Mrs Cooper. Thank you.'

Beryl brushed her hand over Jean's backside, cleaning off the imagined dust as she straightened Jean's skirt.

When Jean turned back to face the Americans, they were leaving. She sighed as the young signal sergeant turned and their gazes locked again. 'I'm Jean Sutton,' she said, her voice quivering with nervousness.

'And I'm Johnny Slade.'

'Well, thanks again.'

'That's ok. Anytime, honey. Say, can I see you later?'

'Later? Why, yes. That would suit,' Jean whispered. 'I finish at ten.'

'I'll be here.'

A worried frown crossed Beryl's brow before she returned to her cash register. *The soldiers always flirted with the girls,* she reflected, *especially the Americans, but none of that had ever led to a rendezvous before.* Beryl consoled herself with the knowledge that she was always there to keep a tight rein on the girls. Any shenanigans on the part of the customers would end in them being ordered out of the café and, if necessary, banned from ever returning. Business being as good as it was, Beryl could afford this policy; it gave her establishment a good reputation with the authorities, and the customers seemed to respect her and her girls even more. But now that Jean had accepted an escort home by a young American soldier, Beryl was left in something of a dilemma. *Should I say something to Jean or Carol? If I told Jean, she might simply ignore my advice.* So, she decided to tell Carol about Jean's arrangement and urge Carol to stay with Jean on their way home.

CHAPTER 2

With the Australian line broken, confusion broke out amid the eerie haze of smoke and mist that was the battlefield. Troops from both sides became hopelessly mixed. The storm that had been threatening all afternoon broke and torrents of rain streamed vertically from the black sky. In next to no time, the ground became sodden and slippery as soldiers fought for a foothold in the mud. This enabled the Australians to slip through the Japanese line and retreat to Kokoda. The Japanese chased them, but eventually broke off the engagement. Under cover of the jungle darkness, the Australians continued their withdrawal and finally regrouped with their main body back at Kokoda. The fresh troops, who had been on their way to reinforce the besieged Australian platoon, were warned by those returning to turn back.

The cool, heavy rain thumping onto his face brought Stan out of his unconsciousness. He felt a heavy weight on his chest, pushing him into the blood-soaked mud around him. As his mind began to focus, he realised a dead body was pressing down on him. There was a ghostly silence surrounding him, broken only by the steady rhythm of the heavy rain. He rolled the body off his chest and stood up. The pain in his head exploded into a constant, sharp pounding. He sank to his knees and closed his eyes, his hand reaching for the back of his head. His scalp had been torn by a severe blow, which, fortunately, had been deflected by his slouch hat. There was bleeding and swelling, but no fracture.

Stan tore off a sleeve from the uniform of a dead soldier. He wrapped it around his head and tied it tight. The pressure eased the bleeding and gave his pounding head some relief. He tried to stand but had to kneel again. He gazed around and saw the limp figures; Japanese and Australians united in death, both having made the ultimate sacrifice for their countries.

A deep sadness engulfed him. All he wanted at that moment was to be back home. Carol was there. Carol was where his heart was, but he knew he could not be there now, not with all this going on. He could not go to Carol, nor could he tell her what he had discovered about his feelings for her. Not when he couldn't be sure if he would ever return home; *and even if I did, would I ever be whole again? After this?*

The thoughts running through his mind had helped to

clear it. He realised that the Japanese may have advanced beyond his present position, and he could be cut off behind their lines. He had no idea how long he had been unconscious. *But why am I alone here? Why didn't the Japanese take their dead? Maybe some were only wounded and looking at me now.* A sudden fear gripped his chest. He looked around in earnest, trying to detect any movement. But there was none, he was alone with the dead.

Why? What was going on? He tried to relax and focus his thoughts. *What should I do next?*

Whenever he felt this way, he always focused on what to do next and that usually got him out of it. He remembered that the Kokoda Track ran along a razor-back mountain range that formed an arc with Kokoda at the middle and proceeded to the spot he was standing on. He had seen this on the maps he had looked at coming up to Kokoda from Port Moresby. He knew that his company would re-form at Kokoda halfway back around the arc to defend the airstrip there. He decided his best chance would be to cut across the Kokoda valley to one of the small native villages, and from there follow the track back to Kokoda. He realised this would not be easy. The terrain would be hellish, and the Japanese might have the same idea to cut off the Australians at Kokoda.

Stan picked up his rifle and checked its bolt action. The magazine was empty, but the rifle worked fine. He searched the dead for ammunition, food and water. He found five live rounds, two tins of bully beef, a few dry biscuits, two bars of dark chocolate, and he filled his canteen with water and another one he had taken from a dead soldier. Suddenly, he heard a movement to his left. He looked around and thought he saw a Japanese soldier taking aim at him, so he dived for cover behind a dead soldier, firing his rifle from his hip as he went down.

Stan thought he might have injured the Japanese soldier because he heard a sharp cry as he dropped to the ground. Looking to the cover of the jungle, he realised there was a three-yard dash in front of him. *Three lousy steps, he thought. Three lousy steps to freedom.* However, it may as well have been three miles. He knew that the Japanese soldier could easily pick him off if he tried to make it. On the other hand, if he stayed where he was, he would surely be captured once the Japanese main body arrived, and he knew what that meant.

Instead, he decided to fight. He took aim in the direction where he had last seen the Japanese soldier. He saw nothing, and immediately dropped his head. The Japanese soldier had not fired. *Did that mean the man was wounded?* His enemy must be alone otherwise others would have fired, but it would not be long before they arrived. The Japanese had the advantage of time. If Stan stayed where he was, sooner or later, they would get him. At that moment, he decided he would not be taken alive. He knew of Australians, who had been captured on Rabaul, tied to trees, and used for bayonet practice. *That won't happen to me*, he vowed, *I'll save the last round for myself.*

*

When the girls left work at 10 pm, the Americans were not there to meet them. Jean stopped to look up and down Queen Street, which was full of soldiers. There were always soldiers around, looking for a drink or a meal, but she didn't see Johnny. Queen Street was in darkness owing to the brownout enforcement as a wartime regulation. The brownout meant that certain sections of the city were lit up while other sections were left in darkness. This was done to confuse Japanese bomber pilots, if they ever came, as they would have difficulty locating their targets.

Carol noticed a few Australian soldiers standing nearby who looked at Jean and started talking softly among themselves. One of them looked like he was going to come over. The two sisters slipped into an awkward silence. Carol eyed the Australians nervously. They were becoming emboldened by Jean's refusal to go with Carol.

'Hello, girlie. You waitin' for someone?' one of them said, sliding up to Jean.

'Yes … I …' Jean stammered.

'If you don't come, Jean, I'll have to go and tell Mrs Cooper,' Carol threatened. Beryl had spoken to them just before they had left. She had made it clear that she expected them to go straight home after work.

Jean laughed. 'You wouldn't do that.'

Carol was about to reply when Jean started jumping up and down. 'They're here. See, I told you Johnny would come. I told you.' Jean began waving and yelling out, 'Johnny! Johnny! Over here, Johnny.'

Johnny looked up and smiled. The two Americans were dressed in newly pressed, cotton-wool-and-synthetic-blended uniforms, which contrasted starkly with the old, ill-fitting World War I woollen Australian uniforms. They walked over to the girls. Jean was beaming with pleasure.

'Bloody Yanks. Take all our women,' vented the Australian standing next to Jean.

'Yeah,' his mate echoed bitterly, 'overpaid, oversexed and over here.'

Johnny glared at the Australian, who locked his jaw and clenched his fists. In an instant, Carol was between them. She extended her hand to the Australian. 'Hello,' she offered, smiling in friendship, 'I'm Carol Sutton and this is my younger sister, Jean.'

Caught by surprise, the Australian stammered, 'Yeah. Ron ... Ron Roberts.'

'It's nice to meet you, Ron,' Carol said, taking his hand and shaking it. 'I know what this must look like, Ron, but it's really quite innocent. You see, my sister and I are terribly afraid to walk home alone this late at night with all the soldiers about. And with the brownout and all, it gets a bit scary for us walking alone in some of the streets. It's awfully dark, you see. Anyway Ron, I hope you can understand that these men are just going to walk us home. For our protection, you understand. That's all.'

'Couldn't ya find any Australians?'

At that question, Johnny tried to get past Carol, who put her arm up to stop him. Frank, the other American signal sergeant, took hold of Johnny's arm and told him to let Carol handle the situation. Johnny shrugged his shoulders. 'Ok,' he said, 'but not for long.'

'What are ya gunna do about it, *Yank?*' Ron said pointedly.

Jean went on, stopping Johnny from replying, or pushing past her. 'Oh. We walk home with Australians too. What really counts is that they understand that they are only walking us home. Nothing more. We must be careful about that. You understand, Ron. Don't you?'

'Yeah. Sure. Say, can I walk you home tomorrow night?'

'Why yes, Ron. Thank you. I'm sure you would be a perfect gentleman about it.'

'Yeah. I would. Only trouble is, we're being shipped out in the mornin'.'

'Oh. That's too bad.'

'Yeah. Righto then,' Ron said, turning back to his mates. 'Come on. Let's go get a beer.'

As they walked away, Ron turned back to see what Carol was doing. She smiled back at him and nodded her head. 'See ya,' he called back.

'Yes. See you, Ron,' she replied.

As Ron and his mates disappeared around the corner, the tension went out of Carol. She put her hand to her forehead and sighed. 'Jean,' she warned, 'one day you're going to get us into serious trouble, and I won't be able to stop it. Why do you always have to make a spectacle of yourself? Why can't you just be a little more reserved and careful about what you do and say?'

'What are you talking about? I didn't start that. It was that bozo. He was the one making all the fuss. Not me.'

'Yes. But can't you see that he reacted to the way you greeted Johnny?'

'Huh? That's my business. Not his. He shouldn't poke his nose in where it's not wanted. And another thing, there's no way I would walk home with that fool of a man. Did you see how he wanted to fight with Johnny?'

'I think Johnny wanted to fight with him too, Jean. They both had quick tempers.'

'Well, that's different. Johnny is with me. He was just trying to protect me.'

Carol raised her hands in frustration. 'I give up,' she whispered. 'Let's go home.'

*

If I'm going to die anyway, I might as well make a dash for it, Stan reasoned.

Without waiting to reconsider, he leapt to his feet and took three lightning strides. The jungle tore at his face and arms as he rushed headlong into the safety of its embrace. Soon he could go no further as he was ensnared in a mass of vines and creepers. Freeing himself from the entanglement, he sank to his knees gasping for air. The shot he had feared had never been fired. *I must have got him,* he thought, *or had I only imagined the whole thing?*

He relaxed and slowed his breathing, calming his racing heart and fear-filled mind. The heavy atmosphere and heat began to affect him; sweat ran down his body and quickly soaked his shirt. He took the canteen from his hip and gulped hard. He drank half of one canteen before he realised it; *I will have to ration myself from now on,* he told himself. The cuts and grazes he had received during his dash through the jungle began to itch, but he resisted the urge to scratch, knowing that scratching a cut could cause it to develop into a tropical ulcer. Then he remembered the wound to his head. It was numb. *Was that a bad thing? Was it already infected?* he wondered.

Deciding there was nothing he could do about that now, he wiped his face and stood back up. He needed to find the valley rim before he could plan his next step, but he was running out of time and light; storm clouds were gathering once again, making it grow darker.

He rushed on, fighting his way through the jumble of greenery in which massive trees were shrouded with clinging vines and creepers. Giant palms with thick thorny edges, ferns and shrubs all fought for precious space and scarce light. All this was punctuated with the cadaverous remains of plant life, which had given up the struggle. He pushed on, hoping he would soon reach the rim, but it did not appear.

Stan began to worry that he was lost, probably circling within the space separating track and rim. He stopped his struggle against the green menace and decided to climb a tall tree to get his bearings. *I simply must find a way to the rim.*

Finding a tall tree, he took off his webbing and laid his rifle on top of it. Next, he reached up and pulled on a vine. It didn't hold, tearing away from its giant host. He tried to get a hold on the tree but found it difficult to climb with the vines entangling him. Finally, he found a vine that held his weight. Wrapping his legs around the vine and locking his feet, he began climbing by pushing with his legs and pulling with his arms. His progress was relatively fast at first, but then fatigue set in, slowing him to a crawl. Inch by gruelling inch, he continued to climb. Now he could use the limbs of the giant hardwood. He wrapped his legs around a firm, large branch and let go of the vine. Using the branches for footing, he continued to fight his way to a clear view of the canopy. Finally, he broke through to the bright light and sky above. Squinting to clear his vision, he gazed out on the endless roll of greenery. Out there, only a short distance away, he saw it. The green canopy disappeared into a chasm of rising mist.

He had been right, and his luck was holding. He looked down and saw a giant pandanus palm growing between the tree and the rim. *That will be my bearing,* he thought. *Now to get down.*

The climb down was just as gruelling as the ascent and by the time he reached the ground his legs were wobbling. Stan smiled as he remembered the walk up from Port Moresby when the Australians were trying to conquer yet another steep descent. The searing pain in their thigh muscles triggered an uncontrollable shaking in their legs, making some soldiers slip on the wet ground.

'Bloody laughing legs!' yelled Billy, Stan's younger mate. After that, 'laughing legs' became a standing joke for anyone who slipped in the mud.

Stan sighed. Only a few days ago they had all been able to laugh together. Now so many of his mates were gone forever and he had to overcome this hellish ordeal alone if he was to survive. He sat down and waited for his energy to return, but realised he was near exhaustion. He took out one of his bars of chocolate and ate it slowly, feeling it settle in his stomach and the energy return to his limbs. His legs finally stabilised, so he gathered his gear and set out for the giant palm marking his way to the edge of the rim. As he went, he marked some trees on their rim side, enabling him to check his progress with an occasional backward glance.

When he finally reached the rim, the darkness of evening was descending on the dimpled trough that was the Kokoda valley. From where he stood, it looked so placid, yet Stan knew he would have to fight every inch of it for a way through. Suddenly, he was again overcome with fatigue. It had taken so much out of him just to find the rim, and there was still so far to go. Fear began to sap his will. *You won't make it,* his mind screamed. *You're going to die here where no one will ever find you.*

Stan sank to the ground and rested his face in his hands. He was alone and afraid. Somehow he had to find the courage to keep going.

Dropping his webbing and weapon, he fell into the embrace of a buttress tree and settled down for the night. He was about to fall into an exhausted sleep when a tropical downpour dumped a torrent of water onto the rainforest. He looked up and saw water teeming from a broad leaf clinging to a vine just above him. The water soaked him through in an instant. He jumped up, took his canteen from the holder on his hip and pulled the cork. In no time it was full of fresh, clean water. *At least I won't go thirsty*, he thought. That thought comforted him as he broke off a palm leaf and sheltered under it until the downpour had ceased.

That night he drifted in and out of a shallow slumber, followed by visions in a re-occurring dream. Carol's smiling face was before him, her bright eyes full of cheer; her face smooth and fresh – so close to him he could smell the lilac-scented soap she always used and feel the gentle breeze on his face that played joyfully with her shoulder-length, bobbed hair.

Suddenly, her smile melted into worried concern, her forehead knotted, and her bright eyes faded and looked down in sorrow. She started to recede, yet she seemed not to move of her own free will, like some mysterious force was pulling her away from him. Her arms opened to him; she looked up at him and tears welled in her eyes, yet she continued drifting further from him. He tried to rush to her but stayed rooted to his spot. Then, a shadow appeared behind her, which seemed to loom over her and embrace her, like some giant eagle that changed into human form, the wings becoming arms, the sharp beak transformed into a sort of peaked cap. Carol lowered her head as she receded further and further into the shadow of the figure's embrace.

Stan tried to run to her, to pull her from the engulfing shadow, but his legs moved in slow motion and he remained where he was, not moving an inch. He tried to call to her, but his voice caught in his throat. He raised his arms, stretching them out, his fingers clutching at air while desperation filled his chest. When she was almost gone from him, he began to rise from a fever-induced slumber, his head shaking, his body shivering, his chest shuddering as he called out Carol's name.

He opened his eyes to the black jungle night and his sweat-soaked body; a raging dryness caught his mouth and throat. He reached for his canteen and swallowed hard as pain throbbed through his brain and the ache in his body pulled him back into a semi-conscious slumber that was his sleep, to eventually dream again the troubled vision, which came to him again … and again … and again.

As Stan sat cradled in the roots of the giant buttress tree, an Australian army messenger left Kokoda for HQ in Port Moresby. In the dispatch case rested two messages from Stan's battalion commander. The first message explained that the Japanese had broken through the battalion's first ambush and were heading for Kokoda. The commander added that his battalion would continue resisting their attacks, but believed the Japanese were a much larger force than army intelligence had predicted, and too large for his soldiers to hold their position at Kokoda. He intended to hold out for as long as he could, then withdraw and fight a staged retreat until more Australian forces could be sent forward. The second message was the list of KIA (killed in action) and MIA (missing in action). Stan's name was on the KIA list because one of the returning soldiers from the ambush had reported that he had seen Stan fall.

CHAPTER 3

One night, when Carol and Jean were walking home from the Victory Café through the dark, browned-out city streets of Brisbane, a rather tall, dark figure began to follow them. He wore a great coat with the collar turned up and a grey hat pulled down over his eyes.

The girls began to walk faster and the figure in the coat kept pace. Carol and Jean were frightened by what was happening, so they began to run, but the figure kept pace with them. The girls stopped and turned to face the person, who had also stopped.

'What do you want?' Carol asked. The figure did not respond. 'Why are you following us?' Still there was no reply.

Maybe it's Dad checking up on us, Carol thought, *to see if we went out with boys on our way home.*

'Dad, if that's you, please tell us now because you are scaring us,' Carol said.

The mystery person took off his hat and moved forward to join them. 'I'm sorry if I scared you, girls,'

Alan said, 'but I had to be sure that you weren't meeting up with some Yanks after work. You know how I don't trust those Yank soldiers.'

'Well, you certainly did scare us,' Jean said sharply. 'I can't believe you would do such a thing, Dad. And anyway, what if we did meet up with some soldiers? What would you do about it?'

'Well, I'd walk with you to see that no harm came to you both.'

'You must be crazy, Dad, if you think that Carol and I can't look after ourselves. If we did walk home with anyone, it would be with someone we could trust.'

'Umm, I'm not so sure about that,' said Alan, turning his hat in his hands. 'Look how scared you were with me following you ...'

'That's different, Dad,' Jean interrupted. 'You scared us because we weren't sure who you were. Anyway, there's two of us and just one of you. If you are that worried about us, why don't you escort us home every night?'

'You know I can't do that. I have to work all hours at the docks, and now with the war on there's more work than ever.'

'So, what happens now?' Carol asked.

'Well, I can see that you were going straight home

after work, so I'm sorry if I caused you any trouble. I guess I'll just have to trust you from now on.'

'That would be a good idea,' Carol said.

They all turned to walk home together, and Alan linked his arms with his daughters. 'You know I love you both, and I don't want anything bad for you.'

'Yes, Dad,' Carol replied. 'And you can trust us. We won't do anything bad.'

Jean remained silent and looked down at her feet as the three of them slowly made their way home.

*

Stan had been drifting in and out of his fever, and when he finally awoke to the stings and bites of ants and parasites all over his body, he realised he had lost track of time. He wondered how long he had been in his fever-induced slumber, but he knew it was longer than just one night. He quickly stripped off and thoroughly brushed himself down. He ended up with welt and bite marks all over his body that burned and itched. He knew not to scratch, however, because he did not want to produce weeping scabs, so he shook out his clothes and redressed.

Next, he took stock of what he had left. He had

his rifle and four rounds of ammunition, one tin of bully beef, a few dry biscuits, one bar of chocolate and two canteens, one half-full of water, the other empty. He knew it would take several days to find his unit on the Kokoda Track. He also knew his food would run out long before he made it back, but whatever his circumstances he knew he had to keep going.

He put on his webbing and started on his journey back out of the wilderness by stumbling his way down the steep slope in front of him. It became so arduous that his legs became tired and started to tremble. Consequently, he took frequent and extended breaks. Also, his unsteady progress was contributing to a growing number of small bruises and minor scratches, which he feared could turn infectious. So, he stopped and rolled his shirt sleeves down. This offered some protection but made him sweat more and increase his thirst. With only a half-canteen of water in his possession, he had to limit his drinking to tiny sips, which did nothing to quell his thirst.

In some places, the undergrowth was so thick that he had to hack his way through with his bayonet. This work cost him his last chocolate bar, and further slowed his progress so much that it took him most of the day just to reach the bottom of the ravine. He arrived there with a terrible headache, but found a stream winding its way down towards the Solomon Sea.

He placed his rifle and webbing on the far bank of the stream, then lowered himself into the cold mountain stream and let it wash over his body. The cold went right through him, and the stings, bites, bruises and scratches disappeared to the cold.

'Ahhhhhhh!' he called out in pleasure. He put his head under the water and felt immediate relief for his headache.

He wanted to stay in the water but forced himself out and let the heat dry his body, although the humidity prevented his clothes from drying. How disappointed he was to feel the pain return. He refilled his canteens and drank as much water as he could, which eventually cleared his headache. He decided to stay the night on the bank of the stream, so he could wash again in the morning before setting out up the mountain. He took the last tin of bully beef out of his pack and ate it. What he would do for food from now on, he had no idea, but he was hopeful of finding his unit before too long.

After having a morning bath in the stream, Stan pushed on up the steep slope. An incredible burning pain set into his legs, and he had to keep telling himself not to stop. He worried that if he stopped, he would not be able to start walking again. Eventually, though, he had to stop. His legs just could not keep going. He ate the last of his biscuits and took a couple of deep swallows of his water. It was at this point that he discarded his rifle and swapped it for a long walking stick, which he cut from a tree with his bayonet. The rifle's weight was just too much for him to carry, and the walking stick gave him leverage to help with his climb. He knew he had to continue on, so he forced himself up and just kept going, one foot after the other, not thinking of anything except simply taking the next step.

During this arduous day, he heard gunfire break out further up the mountain range to his right. He knew the course he was taking was correct and believed he would reach the track behind his own lines. Then he remembered that his mates were fighting the Japanese. It would be difficult for them, so he knew they needed him to be there. He wanted to play his part, and this forced him on with renewed vigour.

It had taken him all day to reach the summit of this ridge, only to find that it was a false peak. He would have to go back down a new ravine and up the other side. He collapsed while staring out at the enormous task in front of him. He wanted to give up the struggle;

to just lay down and not get back up. He was out of food and energy. He had plenty of water, but without food he was doomed. Something deeper, however, kept telling him to go on. His mates needed him; they were greatly outnumbered, and he didn't want the Japanese to capture Port Moresby. If they did, Australia would be wide open, and her shipping lanes vulnerable, which meant Carol and his mum would become captives of the Japanese. He could never let that happen.

Stan slept that night in the open on top of the ridge. He gazed at the night sky, which was brilliantly lit with twinkling stars. The dark blanket of night in this remote location meant there were no other lights to compete with the starlight. *So many beautiful stars.* He realised then why people in ancient times spent so much time studying the stars. *The stars appear so close and so personal in a darkened night.*

That night, Stan did feel part of something much greater than himself. He also knew that he had an immediate personal struggle to navigate in the morning of his next day.

When he awoke it was late in the day, and again he was not sure how long he had been sleeping. He only knew he was exhausted; his body ached and his stomach craved food. Still, he managed to rise and start down the ravine. He knew he would have to find food soon, so he kept a lookout for anything he could eat. It wasn't long before he spotted a shrub with shiny, red currant-like berries. He picked some and rubbed them into the skin on the back of his hand. Then he waited for half an hour to see if his skin reacted to the fruit. When it didn't react, he picked all the red berries on the bush. There were a lot of seeds in the fruit, but he chewed and swallowed only a few of them. It took all his willpower not to gulp them all down. Again, there was no reaction, so he swallowed a few more before making his way down the ravine again, while chewing occasionally on the berries he had gathered.

He reached the bottom of the ravine in the late afternoon and collapsed into the stream that wound its way down the bottom of the ravine. The humidity had drained his body fluids all day and sapped his energy, but worse, it was depleting his precious body salt. Again, the cool of the stream revitalised him. He stayed there so long that he lost any sense of time.

There were tiny fish in the stream that came up to him and sucked on his skin. He took off his hat and held it underwater. The fish went into his hat, so he pulled it up with the fish still inside it. He took the fish out one by one and swallowed them whole. When he had had enough, he got out of the stream and sat on the bank.

He looked at the stream, mesmerised by its movement, then he noticed several snakes crossing the stream. Their movement through the water created a V-shaped wake. He went over to where they slithered out of the water, grabbed one by the tail and smashed its head against a large stone. Drawing out his bayonet, he cut its head off. He did this three times. Next, he peeled the skin from the snakes and gnawed the flesh from their bones. He had eaten so much that he felt a little nauseous. *Imagine that,* he thought, *just a short time ago I was ravenous.*

He fell into a deep, contented sleep, and awoke the next morning refreshed and ready to start the climb, which was gradual. He was revived from the food and rest from the previous day, so his mind wandered to Carol. He so much wanted to see her and tell her the things he had been wanting to tell her for some time now, and for the first time since he started his journey, he felt there was a real chance that he might see her again.

The rest of the day was spent climbing up the mountain ridge, fighting his way through the rainforest that in places continued to tear at his clothing and skin. The scratches on his body were turning into angry, red welts that burned and itched so much that he had to use all his willpower to avoid scratching them. Nevertheless, he did rub them only to find that that made them itch even more.

He pushed on and on, reaching the summit only to find it was another false peak, and the next stage was the largest one of all. The ravine was deep, and the rise was steep and rugged. He sat down, exhausted and disillusioned. *How do I know if this is the last ravine I have to cross? Would it really matter if I gave up now?* he wondered. *What could I do even if I reunited with my unit?*

He knew that the Japanese were numerous and well-armed, while the Australians were few and ill-equipped. *Wouldn't I just die in the line anyway?* He was at the point of giving up, when he heard another battle break out on the next ridge. It was closer to him now. He knew for certain that this would be the last ravine he would have to overcome, and if he was to reach his mates fighting on the line he would have to move now.

With renewed vigour he set out down the slope, moving as fast as he could. He stumbled a few times but did not let his unsteady legs slow him down. *Soon,* he thought, *very soon, I will be out of this wilderness and back with my unit.*

Even when the light faded and darkness set in, he

tried to keep going, but realised it was too dangerous. He could slip and sprain an ankle, or even break a leg, so he stopped for the night and slept on the side of the slope.

At first light the next day he was up and moving. Eventually, he reached the bottom of the ravine, but did not stop to rest. He knew he had to hurry, if he was going to meet up with his mates. *I will climb this ridge and I will rejoin my unit,* he told himself over and over as he pushed on and on up the ridge. One cruel grinding step after another. *One more step … one more step,* he kept telling himself.

Finally, he stopped and fell to the ground exhausted. His energy was gone, his will to succeed almost finished. He had drained a whole canteen of water just to get to this point, which left him with only one more for the rest of the climb. His head ached and throbbed; his legs shook constantly like jelly, but he knew he had to go on somehow. At this point, it occurred to him that he would have to take a diagonal line to his left for this last effort – just in case the Japanese had advanced, making him come out behind their lines. This would mean even more distance for him to cover. He sighed and pulled himself up with his walking stick. *One more effort – just once more,* he told himself.

As he got to his feet, he realised he had been sitting next to a pandanus palm that had large, dark orange-yellow fruit that was breaking apart in its ripeness. He picked the fruit and chewed it raw. It had an oily, nutty taste, and he devoured as much as his stomach could take.

He stepped off for his last effort. The diagonal line made it easier for him to climb, and he was grateful for the relief he felt. At last, he burst through the jungle and stepped onto the Kokoda Track. It was so narrow he had almost walked right over it. He sat down to gather his thoughts and get his bearings. He had made it through against all odds. Relief flooded through him. He knew he would have to keep moving along the track if he was going to rejoin his unit. If he waited too long, the advance guard of the Japanese might catch up with him.

Stan heard noises of soldiers coming along the track, so he slipped into the jungle out of sight. It was some of the men from his own unit. He called out to them; then came out from hiding. His clothes were so tattered and torn, and he was so thin that he was not recognised at first, but he soon saw his mate, Billy Bowen.

Billy was younger than Stan, and the two of them had struck up a friendship on the walk up from Port Moresby. Billy was friendly, always making jokes and horsing around. He was handsome with thick, black, curly hair and clear blue eyes. He had a larrikin streak that made the others laugh. Although a little shorter than average in height, he was comfortable with that, and didn't try to force himself on others.

'It's me, Billy. Stan. You know, we came up the track together,' mumbled Stan.

'My god, Stan. It is you. Look at you. Where ya been, cobber?'

Stan was speechless. He just gazed at the familiar faces, his eyes welling up.

'Here, mate. It's all right. You're with us now,' Billy said, moving up to Stan and putting his hand on his shoulder. 'Let me give you a hand, mate,' he added, taking his hand from Stan's shoulder and putting it under his armpit. The others came in around him, allowing him to rest on their shoulders before they started walking back along the track.

'We're moving back to Isurava. We'll hit them again from there,' Billy said.

Stan didn't say anything; he let his mates do all the talking while he tried to walk as best he could. They told Stan that they couldn't hold the Japanese at Kokoda and had only just escaped. They laughed when they related to Stan that the Japanese had attacked Kokoda in the early hours of the morning, which was thick with fog, and when the time came for them to escape, they simply walked backwards through the advancing Japanese line.

'After that, we got orders to retake Kokoda. What a stupid bloody order. Didn't they realise we had just been driven out of there?' Billy remarked. 'I tell you, Stan. Those blokes back in Moresby have no idea what we are going through up here. Of course, we failed. All that achieved was that we lost good men we could ill afford to lose.'

Billy told Stan that they had to withdraw from Oivi and Deniki because of repeated, determined attacks from the Japanese and the fear of encirclement. He also said that they had lost their CO in the heavy fighting at Deniki. He went on to explain that they had learnt how to hold the line just long enough before withdrawing to avoid the Japanese cutting off their escape down the narrow Kokoda track to their next defensive position.

Eventually, they arrived at Isurava. Billy took Stan to the company aid post where a medic treated his wounds and abrasions, which had all become infected. They were washed in hot water and antiseptic and dusted with sulphonamide powder.

The doctor looked at him. 'You can go back to Moresby.'

'No, Doc. I want to rejoin my unit. I can still fight,' Stan insisted.

'I know you're needed, young man, but you really are pretty sick,' the doctor replied.

'Please, Doc. Can't you just give me something?'

'What you really need is rest and nourishment.'

'I'll rest when I get back in the line, and I can eat what you can give me.'

'Ummm …'

'Please, Doc.'

'You also have a fever.'

'Aspirin and penicillin?'

'I can give you some tablets to take, and you can get some bully beef from the kitchen.'

'Thanks, Doc.'

'Well, I hope I'm doing right by you.'

'Don't worry, Doc. You are as far as I am concerned.'

*

A little over a week after Frank and Johnny had walked Carol and Jean home, Carol was sitting on Stan's mum's front porch. They were talking about Stan. Carol asked Esmay if she had heard from him.

'Not for a long time, dear,' Esmay replied. 'I suspect

it's difficult to get the mail through.'

'Yes,' replied Carol. 'I'm sure that's the reason.'

They sat together for a while, not saying anything – just looking out at the street in front of the house. Then Carol broke the silence. 'Mrs Taylor, has Stan ever said anything to you about me?'

'Oh yes, dear. He is always talking about you. In his last letter he asked after you.'

'What did he say?'

'Well. Let's see. He asked how you were, and what you were doing. If you had anyone special in your life now.'

'So, you think he likes me? Wants me to wait for him?'

'Well. Yes, dear. I suspect he does. I'm surprised he hasn't said anything to you.'

'I always got the feeling that he liked me, but he never said anything. I just assumed he only wanted us to be friends.'

'Well, I can't interfere with matters of the heart. Why don't you write to him and ask him how he feels about you, dear?'

'Should I do that? Should I be the one to do that?'

'Probably not quite the correct etiquette, but if I were you I would. I suspect you'll be happy with his reply.'

Just then, a telegram delivery boy arrived and came

up to the porch. Esmay rose unsteadily to meet him, accepted the telegram and signed for it. Shaking, she opened the telegram and read it. She gasped, then stumbled and collapsed into a crumpled heap. Holding onto the porch railing, Esmay sat up, staring out onto the street.

Carol rushed to her side. 'What's wrong Mrs Taylor? Are you all right?'

Esmay said nothing, simply handed Carol the telegram. It was from the Australian Government advising her that Stan had been killed in the service of his country and offering her their condolences. Carol sat down next to Esmay and put her arms around her. The two women began to cry.

*

On their way back to his unit, Billy told Stan that the now-deceased CO had listed him as KIA, so Stan went to see the battalion commander. 'Yes, Stan. That notice went out over a week ago. Your next of kin would have been notified by now. I'll send a new dispatch advising that you have returned to active duty.'

Stan now realised that he had indeed lost track of some days on his journey back to his unit. 'Well, Sir. I wish you wouldn't,' he said. 'If I get killed and you have to send another notice to my mum, she'll have to go through all the heartache again, and the odds of my getting killed are pretty high. Right?'

'Yes. You have a point, Stan, but I must notify Moresby about your returning to active duty. Besides, you want to get paid for all this fighting, don't you? Tell you what, I will ask them not to notify your mother until you see them personally. How does that sound?'

'That's good, Sir. If I survive this, it will be a great surprise for both me and Mum,' Stan said with a smile.

'Good lad. Now report to your company commander.'

Stan was assigned to Billy's trench, and together they dug it deep enough to kneel in without their heads being above ground level. After that, they waited for the Japanese to attack, and Stan relayed to Billy his adventure in the wilderness. Billy was impressed, and asked what snake tasted like.

'Umm … kind of like chicken but a bit saltier. Remember I had to eat it raw,' Stan said.

'Oh yeah. Talking about salt. Have you taken your salt tablet yet?' Billy asked.

'No, I don't have any.'

'Not to worry. Have one of mine. The doc says we need to take them because we sweat so much up here.

A couple of the lads got cramps and passed out. They didn't have enough salt in their bodies. So now we all take one salt tablet a day.'

'Ok. Thanks, Billy. By the way, what's with the bloody awful food we get? Do we ever get anything besides Anzac biscuits or bully beef to eat?'

'Well, we do get chocolate and tea and sugar when it's not spoiled. You know, Stan, that's better than what we used to get around here. All we used to have in the mornings was a dingo's breakfast.'

'What's that?' Stan asked.

'A scratch, a fart and a sniff around.' They both laughed.

'Actually, the only way we can get supplies through is with air drops a long way back down the track, and the fuzzy-wuzzy angels have to carry it all the way up from there, and then the poor buggers carry out our seriously wounded all the way to Moresby. They do a bloody marvellous job for us, mate, so I guess we shouldn't complain too much.'

'What's a fuzzy-wuzzy angel?'

'Oh. They're the local native porters. They work for next to nothing, and they slog their hearts out for us. I tell you, mate, when this is over, we'll owe them a great debt of gratitude.'

They went into a silence and scanned the rainforest for any movement. There was a shallow creek directly in front of them and a small vegetable garden, which the natives tended, but not this day. In the background was the dense rainforest. The distance from their foxhole to the rainforest was no further than eighty yards. They were on a rise, so they held the higher ground, which was to their advantage.

Stan knew that his battalion would make the Japanese pay for any ground they took, but the real question was: *Could they hold out until the regular soldiers arrived?* The regular soldiers had returned from fighting in the Middle East and were now walking up the Kokoda Track to relieve them.

When the fighting did come, it was preceded by a bombardment from a cannon that the Japanese had stripped, carried up the track, and reassembled. The bombardment did not do much damage to the Australians, however, who huddled in their foxholes away from danger. Only a direct hit could harm them, and that was rare. The Australians knew that when the cannon stopped firing, the Japanese would attack. It did eventually stop and the Japanese broke through the rainforest and assaulted the trenches, screaming *Banzi!* They raced forward in groups of about one hundred, which made easy targets for the Australians.

By this time, the Australians had been supplied with Bren and Owen guns, which were more efficient and deadly than their WWI weapons. A frontal assault like this, with men charging into machine guns and automatic fire, was not the attack method used by modern armies. However, the Japanese commander rightly believed that the Australians were few and that he could crush them in one decisive blow, leaving the way open to Port Moresby. He used this tactic because he was trying to keep to a very tight timetable. His supply lines were now stretched, and vital supplies were not getting through from Buna, their supply base on the north side of New Guinea. The allied air force, stationed in Port Moresby, was beginning to sink the Japanese ships coming from Rabaul, which were carrying supplies and reinforcement troops.

The Japanese commander was not counting on the Australian tenacity and rugged fighting spirit. Even when it came down to close quarter and hand-to-hand fighting, the Australians did not yield. They continued to fight with a determination to win.

The fighting that day went on from daybreak to dusk. Time after time the Japanese assaulted, and time after time they were driven back. The Japanese officers, who stood behind their soldiers, told them to *Attack, Attack!*, so wave after wave of Japanese soldiers rushed forward into murderous gunfire.

At one point in the battle, the Japanese reached Billy and Stan's trench. They used the butt of their weapons as clubs and thrust their bayonets into Japanese chests. One Japanese soldier fell onto Billy and bit a chunk out of his cheek, and in return Billy bit the bottom half of his enemy's ear off. Such was the nature of the uncompromising determination to win from both sides. Stan and Billy were saved from certain death when a HQ platoon rushed to their aid and drove the Japanese back.

When the last assault had been repelled, Billy and Stan collapsed back into their trench and stared out at the wicked scene in front of them. 'My god, Stan,' Billy said, 'did we really do that?'

'Yes, mate, and we'll have to do it again and again,' Stan replied.

Japanese soldiers lay scattered in front of them; in some places three deep. Billy counted one hundred and five dead Japanese men, but he gave up after that – there were just too many, and the Japanese had carried their wounded and some of their dead from the battlefield, so it was impossible to get an accurate number.

That night, the regular soldiers arrived and took up their positions. Although they had been officially relieved of duty at the front, Stan's battalion asked to stay on. They knew it was going to be hard on those who stayed. It was finally agreed that the two groups would unite for the battle that would surely come in the morning.

*

After Frank and Johnny had walked them home in the browned-out city of Brisbane, Carol did not hear from Frank for some time, so she assumed that he did not want to see her again. He had been very polite and friendly on the walk home, so she had confused feelings about him. On the one hand, she had wanted to see him again, but on the other hand, she was happy that she didn't have to make a decision about him. Johnny had seen Jean almost every day.

One day, Frank and Johnny came into the café together.

'I'm sorry I haven't been able to see you before this, Carol,' Frank said, 'but I was called away on a mission. I haven't been in Brisbane. I hope you haven't forgotten me?'

'Oh no, I haven't. Frank, isn't it?'

But Carol was not telling him the whole truth. The fact was that she was trying to forget him. He had made an impression on her, but she still felt that she was being disloyal to Stan by thinking about Frank. *It was silly really,* she thought, *but there is something unspoken between me and Stan, something that his death has not yet taken away from me.* Carol sometimes felt that Stan had been trying to be candid with her, but something had been standing in the way of him telling her how he really felt about her. Although nothing had been stated between them, she still felt she had needed to wait for Stan to say it, and now Stan had been killed and Frank had come back and complicated it again. Being so close to Stan's death, Carol had not had sufficient time to grieve and get over the terrible news.

'Yes, that's right. Look Carol, could I walk you home again tonight?'

It was said with so much earnestness that she replied without any thought. 'Yes, of course. Oh, I mean …'

'Great, I'll see you at ten. You still finish at ten, right?'

'Ummm … yes. At ten.'

He was gone almost as fast as he had appeared. And there it was. She stood there confused and anxious as she watched him disappear into the bright light streaming through the doorway.

'Hey, girlie. How about taking our order now that your *Yank* has gone?'

'What?' There it was again. The way the word *Yank* was spoken – as if it had been spat from the mouth. Like it was something bitter that needed removing.

'My order?'

'Oh, yes. Sorry, Sir. What was it you wanted?'

The rest of Carol's shift was one long evening of confusion that didn't end when she left the café at ten with Frank.

CHAPTER 4

During the lull in fighting, after the regular soldiers had arrived, Billy took time to attend to the hole in his cheek. He went to the field ambulance and a medic gave him some iodine in a small bottle and told him to apply it three times a day. When the medic applied the first application, it gave such a nasty sting that it made Billy yell loudly. Back in the trench, he showed Stan the iodine and asked if he would apply it in future because he did not trust himself to do it regularly.

Since the Australians were making a more determined effort to hold their position, the Japanese decided to make a greater effort to encircle them and cut off their retreat, while crushing them with frontal attacks of waves of Japanese soldiers, 200 at a time. The soldiers who circled around behind the Australians, however, ran into the rear guard of Australian regular soldiers coming up from Port Moresby. After fierce fighting, the Japanese retreated, leaving the way open for a future Australian withdrawal.

At first light, the Japanese again attacked the

Australians through the vegetable garden in front of Billy and Stan, but they could not crack the Australian defences. With the enemy so close, the Australians from their vantage point were able to inflict severe punishment on their enemy. The smell of cordite filled the air, the smoke of battle hung close, and the water from the previous night's rain still filled their trench and lay in muddy pools around them, forcing them to suffer the mud while continuing to fight. The Australians were a mixed bunch of fresh, new regular soldiers, who had just arrived at the battlefield, and other citizen soldiers, who had not had any relief for weeks, and it was beginning to show. The citizen soldiers had not had enough sleep, most were suffering from malaria and dysentery, and they had not changed their socks in weeks, which meant the skin on their feet had begun to rot.

Nevertheless, Stan and Billy stood resolute, not willing to give ground. Eventually, however, the numbers started to tell and the company beside Stan's position started to crack. At this point, Stan witnessed an incredible act of bravery. One Australian soldier, with Bren gun blazing from his hip rushed forward, screaming as he went. The Japanese became so bewildered that they withdrew. When it quietened down, the Australian soldier who had rushed forward was shot dead by a Japanese sniper.

It all happened so fast that Stan and Billy had difficulty taking it all in. Not long after that, the Australians were ordered back to Alola.

After arriving at Alola, Stan and Billy were ordered to report to the medical officer, who ordered them back to the hospital in Port Moresby. Stan's head wound had turned into a tropical ulcer, and he had malaria, which triggered convulsions. His dysentery caused him to lose half his body weight. Billy's condition was much the same as Stan's.

*

Frank and Carol left the café promptly at ten. Jean had been on the morning shift and had left with Johnny at two. Carol and Jean were on different shifts because Lucy, another waitress and friend of Jean's, had swapped shifts with her. Carol didn't like the idea of Jean being alone with Johnny, but she went along with it because Jean and Lucy would have caused a scene, which would not have pleased Beryl.

Frank handed Carol a tin of canned ham and another of turkey. 'I didn't know which one you would like,' he said, 'so I got you one of each.'

'Yes, Frank. I like them both. Thank you.'

Carol knew how much the Australian soldiers hated the fact that American soldiers had access to cheap luxury goods like nylon stockings and canned meat through their postal exchange (PX), to which Australians had no access. *It must be galling for Australian soldiers to see the reaction of young Australian women towards Americans in their gratitude for receiving such luxury items. Holding hands, embracing, and even kissing in public, something that would have been unthinkable before the war,* she thought.

'Say, do you have to go home right away?' Frank asked.

'No. Did you want to go somewhere?'

'Well, my unit has a party going on at Cloudland. Would you like to go?'

'Sure,' replied Carol. 'I haven't been to Cloudland since you Americans took it over.'

'Yes … Sorry about that, but we are storing sensitive equipment there that needs special care. I hope you Australians don't mind too much.'

'Ummm … well, just for the war.'

'Oh sure. You'll get it back soon enough.'

They ran to catch a tram, which took them up Queen Street to the front of the National Hotel (which had become an American bar), into Wickham Terrace, across Brunswick Street in the Valley, past the Valley

Baths and into Breakfast Creek Road at Newstead. Cloudland's distinct parabolic arch atop Montpellier Hill was visible long before they got there.

'What sort of equipment do you store up there?' Carol asked, then checked herself. 'Oh … sorry. That's classified, right? Loose lips sink ships, and all that. You've probably told me too much already.'

'Yes, I guess I have. But how do you know I'm not spinning a yarn to make myself seem important?'

'Oh no … I don't think you …' Carol checked herself because she didn't want Frank to think she had feelings for him, but then she felt her ears start to burn.

'Say, are you blushing?'

'Oh dear.' Carol averted her face away from Frank.

'Well, you must really like me. I didn't know what to think after our last date …'

'Well, it wasn't a date. Remember?' Carol interrupted. 'You just walked me home.'

'Yes, I know. But you seemed so stiff and proper. I didn't think you liked me. I had to work up my courage to see you again.'

'I see. And that's why you took so long?'

'Yes. I wasn't really sent anywhere. I'm sorry. I made that up, but the truth was embarrassing.'

'I can see that. But I hope you will always tell me the

truth in future.'

'Oh sure. You can count on it.'

The tram stopped and they got off. They got on another open-air Alpine tram, which ran up the 330-feet, steep Montpellier hillside. As the tram ascended, Carol and Frank took in the view of the wharfs and the Brisbane River. The lights were on down at the wharfs, which meant the men were working. *That's a good thing*, Carol thought. *At least Dad won't be home worrying about Jean and me.*

The tram stopped at the rear entrance to Cloudland. The cool breeze from the river made Carol shiver and run her hands up and down the tops of her arms.

'You're cold,' Frank said, and he put his arm around her, pulling her close to him.

'Oh …' Carol said, but she did not resist him.

The twinkling lights from the wharfs gave the appearance of a fairyland. Carol gave in to the moment and snuggled into Frank's chest. She felt guilty – because of her dad, because of Stan, because of Jean. Then she felt angry that she felt guilty. *After all, it's my life, and I'm an adult.* All these thoughts left her confused about her feelings.

Frank turned Carol to face him and bent down to kiss her. At the last moment, Carol turned away, and

Frank's kiss rested on her cheek. 'Is something wrong?' Frank asked.

'Ummm … Frank, it's a bit too fast for me. Can we take it a little slower?'

'Yes. Sure. But we may not have much time before I get posted away. I am being truthful this time. Some highly qualified guys are arriving in about three weeks' time, so Johnny and I might get posted out.'

'Well, I don't see how that should make a difference, really. We can still be good friends without becoming too intimate.'

Frank turned away and looked out over the wharfs. Carol was still in his arms, and she did not make any move to break away. The silence held out for a few minutes, but they were minutes that seemed like a lifetime to Carol. Finally, Frank said, 'Yes. We can. But is kissing too intimate?'

'It's not the kissing that worries me, Frank. It's what comes after the kissing. Maybe when I'm surer of you and myself. Would that do, Frank?'

Carol was wanting Frank to say 'yes', even though a 'no' would be much less messy for her, allowing her to make a clean break from him.

'Oh, yes. Of course. But are you sure there is nothing else holding you back?'

'Well, there is Dad and Johnny and Jean …'

'Why? What does it have to do with them?' Frank interrupted.

'It has a lot to do with them, Frank. I must set a good example for Jean. She is my younger sister, and I don't want to see her hurt, and I don't want to hurt my father either. He has already suffered so much from losing Mum. He also has a hard time with his work and his drinking. I don't want to do anything that might tip him over the edge. We all depend so much on each other.'

'Ok Carol. I see it now, but I must warn you. I'm the type that only has one girl for life. If you become that girl, I'll always want you with me.'

There was a pause after that, and Carol wondered for a moment what Frank was trying to tell her. She was about to ask him, when he suddenly let her go from his arms and took her by the hand. 'Come on,' he said. 'Let's go inside.'

They entered Cloudland through the rear entrance. Inside, Carol saw the huge stockpile of American equipment. It was impressive, taking up almost the entire floor space and stacked almost to the high ceiling.

'Wow!' Carol exclaimed. 'So much equipment. I think you were telling me the truth, Frank. This *is* a stockpile of sensitive equipment.'

'Yes. It's all for signals. To keep us in contact with the war up north and the Pentagon back home. But don't worry, Carol. All this will be gone by tomorrow. We are moving to a permanent location to set up all this equipment, so you knowing about it now won't worry us.'

'Oh, of course. I didn't want to know anyway, but it is nice to know more about you, Frank. So, you are a radio operator?'

'Well, something like that.'

They drifted past the piles of equipment and entered a small portion of the dance floor that was clear. There were a few other signalmen there already with their dates. Carol saw Jean and Johnny, so they walked over to join them.

'Carol, isn't this great? Johnny has been teaching me the jitterbug and the boogie,' Jean said excitedly.

Carol noticed that the others were dancing the latest dance craze from America. They had a turntable and a collection of Glen Miller and the Andrew Sisters records, which they were playing.

'I can teach you too, if you want, Carol,' Johnny offered.

Carol looked at Frank. This seemed like a good opportunity to learn the jitterbug, and her expression showed it.

'Go ahead, Carol. I'm not much of a dancer,' Frank said. 'I'll look after Jean.'

'I don't need looking after, Frank, but I will stay with you if you ask me nicely.'

Frank obliged and Jean smiled. 'You're a nice guy, Frank,' she said.

Carol couldn't help noticing the change in Jean. She was more confident. More mature than when she had first met Johnny.

'This is a great dance floor,' Johnny said. 'When we were storing all this equipment, we felt how it bounces. Feels like it's built on springs or something.'

'That's why we like it so much. We used to hold dances and balls here before it became your storehouse.' They drifted into silence, concentrating on the dance moves. 'Do you think there will be dances here after your equipment is removed?' Carol asked.

'Sure, there will be … lots of us want it, and it's good for our morale.'

Everything seems to be about the war effort and the Americans, Carol thought, but she checked herself from saying anything because she didn't want to offend Johnny.

They played *Pennsylvania 6-5000,* and *Chattanooga Choo Choo.* By this stage, Carol's dancing had improved.

'Say, you're a fast learner,' Johnny said. Carol returned his smile. The music stopped and they switched to the Andrew Sisters' 1941 hit song, *Boogie Woogie Bugle Boy of Company B*.

'Carol, can I dance this one with Jean?'

'Yes. It's time I went back anyway.'

Johnny was already leaving the dance floor before Carol had time to catch her breath, and Jean rushed out to join him. Carol took her time returning to Frank while admiring how accomplished Johnny and Jean appeared. They seemed so natural dancing together.

'They do look good together,' Carol remarked to Frank, but she was really concerned that they may have become too close in such a short space of time.

'Yes, they do,' Frank replied.

Carol went on thinking that Jean and Johnny might get hurt, dancing so fast. Johnny was throwing Jean around from hip to hip and then lifting her up in the air upside down; her dress was falling to her hips revealing her underpants. The others on the dance floor stopped to watch them. Carol was about to go over to stop them, when the music stopped, and they came over to join her.

Carol smiled. 'You two certainly put on a show for everyone,' she said, 'but did you have to show so much, Jean? I could see your underpants.'

Jean laughed. 'Oh, that's ok. They're a clean pair!'

Rather than push her point, Carol decided to let it slide and talk to Jean when they returned home, but now she was really concerned about Jean's relationship with Johnny. She hoped she could trust in the judgement of her sister, but she was beginning to doubt if she could.

'Can I get you a soda?' Frank asked, interrupting Carol's thoughts.

'What?' Carol asked, regaining her concentration.

'A soda. Can I get you one?'

'Oh. Yes, please.'

Frank walked across the dance floor and left Carol alone with Jean and Johnny. Carol took the opportunity to say something to both of them. 'Now that we are alone, Jean, I need to tell you and Johnny that I think you are getting too seriously involved with each other. You don't seem to understand that what you did just now was too much.'

'Say, what are you? Jean's mother or her sister?' Johnny replied.

'Actually, Johnny, I am both. You see, we lost our mother when Jean was born, and I have been trying to look after her ever since.'

'Well, you don't have to look after me anymore,' Jean

said angrily. 'I'm quite capable of looking after myself, thank you very much.'

'Oh, Jean. Please don't be angry with me. I'm only trying to help you.'

'Well, I don't need your help either. If Johnny and I want to dance like that, we will, and there is nothing you can do to stop us. You're beginning to sound like Dad, and he can't stop me either. Come on Johnny, let's dance some more.'

With that said, they both left Carol standing alone and walked to the dance floor, where Johnny took Jean in his arms and danced with her close to him. After a short dance, they slipped outside.

Carol was distraught. *What can I do?* Just then, Frank returned with her soda and Carol told him what had happened, and that she was worried about them being alone outside.

'Oh, I see. That's why they went outside. Well, I could tell them that I have to take the two of you home now. I can use the company Jeep outside, but I really think you are making something out of nothing, Carol. A lot of people in the US dance like that, but I'll go and get them if you like.'

'No. Maybe you are right. If I get involved again now, Jean will do something silly. Let them have a little time together. You can go and get them later, if they have not returned.'

'Ok. By the way, I think you are doing the right thing.'

Not long after that, Johnny and Jean came back inside. Then, Frank and Johnny escorted the women out to the Jeep that was assigned to Frank's unit.

Back home, Carol would not allow Frank to kiss her goodnight. Instead, she shook his hand and told him that she had had a wonderful night. She hoped her example would be taken up by Jean, but just the opposite happened. Johnny took Jean in his arms, and they gave each other a lingering kiss. Carol looked away.

'Can I see you again tomorrow, Carol?' Frank enquired.

'Yes, ok,' Carol replied, without really thinking.

'Careful you two,' Jean said with a smile on her face. 'Next thing you know you'll be falling in love.'

Carol looked at Jean in disgust.

'I like you, Carol. I like you a lot,' Frank said, looking directly into Carol's eyes. He winked and smiled at her; then, Frank and Johnny jumped into the Jeep and they left. Carol and Jean stood waving and watched them leave.

When they got inside, Carol turned to face Jean. 'You really have to stop this, Jean,' she began.

'No. You stop, Carol. Stop trying to control me.'

'But can't you see that your kiss tonight was not appropriate. You haven't known Johnny anywhere near long enough to be kissing like that. Are you sure you know what you're doing? I don't want anything bad for you, Jean. You know that. Right?' Carol said with a conciliatory tone.

'Yes. I know that, Carol,' Jean replied with a softer tone. 'You are my big sister after all, but you really don't have to worry. It's just that Johnny makes me feel alive. I love being with him.'

'Oh dear. I hope you know what you are getting yourself into, Jean.'

'Yes, dear sister, I do, and it's wonderful.'

CHAPTER 5

'Do you love me, Johnny?' Jean asked.

'Sure, I do, Baby. You're my sweet little angel.'

'Am I, Johnny? Am I really your angel?'

'Sure.'

Johnny got out of bed and took a packet of cigarettes from the pocket of his uniform, which lay crumpled on the floor. He lit up and walked over to the grime-covered window of the cheap South Brisbane hotel and opened it. The view was of a solid brick wall, which formed part of a building housing a steam-cleaning business.

Roughly 80,000 American troops were in Brisbane, which had an estimated population of only 335,000. Brisbane had become a segregated city with African-Americans restricted to South Brisbane. Johnny had a special pass that allowed him to collect items and personnel from the South Brisbane Station, which was as far as trains from interstate could go due to the different railway gauge used by the New South Wales and Queensland governments. Johnny knew that no one in South Brisbane would recognise him or Jean, and that was why he brought her here.

'Johnny, can I ask you something?' Jean asked, sitting up in the bed and allowing the sheet to fall to her lap.

'Sure, Baby. What is it?'

'Why do your Black soldiers have to stay in South Brisbane? Why can't they come over to our side of the river?'

'That's just the rule. I guess they're different from us,' he said, turning and facing her.

'How? How are they different?'

'I don't know. They just are.' Johnny paused for a moment while he thought about it. Then he continued, 'Maybe it's because they can't be trusted. You know. They might start trouble. Why? Does it bother you?'

'Well, it doesn't seem right. Do you think it's right, Johnny?'

'I don't know. It's just the way it is, so why worry about it? Don't you keep your Blacks separated from the rest of you?' He took a deep drag on his cigarette and let the smoke escape slowly from his slightly opened mouth. The smoke rose slowly, covering his face and forcing him to close his eyes before rising further and dissipating into the clear air above his head.

'No. We never have. It's not one of our rules. Carol

told me that we should treat the Aborigines better, but we never separated them from the rest of us. She also said something about segre … umm. What's the word, Johnny?"

'Segregation.'

'Yes, that's it. She was complaining about it. She said we have never been a segregated society, so why do we allow it now?'

'Well, there's nothing we can do about it, so why worry about it? Let's just drop it,' snapped Johnny, somewhat annoyed by Jean's criticism of his country.

'Oh. I didn't mean to upset you, Johnny. You still love me, don't you?'

'Sure, Baby. Sure,' he said, turning back to the window and flicking his cigarette through it. He watched the sparks fly from it as it smashed into the brick wall outside. He returned to the bed. 'Want one?' he asked, offering the packet to Jean.

'Do you want me to have one, Johnny?'

'Do what you want, Baby. I'm not your boss.'

She shook her head. 'Don't you want to be my boss? I love you so much. You can be my boss if you want.'

Johnny laughed. 'That's great, Baby. Let's just say you're happy to keep me happy.'

'Oh! I am, Johnny. I surely am.'

Johnny tossed the packet on top of his ruffled uniform and sat down on the edge of the bed with his back to Jean, who rose and knelt on the bed behind him. She wrapped her arms around him and pressed her head into his back.

'Stay with me, Johnny. Please don't ever leave me,' she pleaded.

'Now what's all this about? We have a good time. Don't we?'

'Oh! Yes. We do. I always have a good time with you.'

'Well then. Just drop all this *don't ever leave me* stuff.'

'Oh Johnny, I didn't mean anything by it, really. I know we will always be happy. I just wanted you to know how much I love you,' she said, releasing her grip and raising her head.

'That's right. We are happy together.'

She held up Johnny's arm and looked at his watch. 'Gosh, look at the time,' she said. 'I have to get goin' now or I'll be late for work.' Jean rose and got dressed in a hurry, not bothering with her make-up. Johnny offered to drop her at the café, so they left in his Jeep.

When they got to the Victory Café, Carol noticed them arrive. She also noticed that Jean had not made-up her face, which was something Jean always took particular care in doing. 'Where did you go with,

Johnny?' Carol asked as Jean hurried to tie on her apron.

'Oh, he just took me for a ride.'

'Where did you go?'

'Out to Mount Coot-tha. We were in a hurry to get back.'

Carol was still worried about Jean but let the matter drop. She was seeing Frank regularly now, but his serious nature kept them on an even keel as far as romance was concerned. Carol had never felt pressured by him, and hoped it was the same for Jean and Johnny.

*

Later that week, Frank took Carol to a private function in the enlisted men's quarters at Newstead House. The function room was small with fold-out crepe paper and coloured lights strung from the ceiling. In the centre of the ceiling was a Christmas bell from which all the streamers looped out to the surrounding walls. Even though it was not Christmas, the decorations added a festive atmosphere to the function. It was a small affair, but Carol was impressed by the effort that the American soldiers had gone to in setting up for a happy evening. She also wondered where the decorations had come from, since the war time restrictions were in full swing. So many Americans were in Brisbane now, and they all seemed to have so much more than the Australians.

Again, there was the usual big-band sounds of Glen Miller playing on a phonogram in the corner of the room, so Carol and Frank took to the floor along with all the others. After a few dances, Frank asked Carol if she would like to see the park that surrounded Newstead House.

She agreed, so they stepped out into the cool evening of a hot summer's day. The breeze was coming up from the Brisbane River, and as it played with Carol's light blouse, she felt a sudden relief that flooded through her body. She closed her eyes and breathed in the smell of a fresh-cut lawn. *More attention to detail*, she thought. Carol noticed Frank's newly pressed uniform, his polished black shoes, and his holstered .45. *He's every inch a soldier.*

'Do you like it here?' Frank asked.

'Oh yes. It is delightful,' she replied.

Frank sat down on the high side of the riverbank and Carol sat down next to him.

'Strange, isn't it?' Frank asked. 'This war has brought me halfway around the world to find you.'

'Yes. That's a happy co-incidence, I suppose.'

'Umm … Tell me, Carol. What do you see in your future?'

'Oh, I don't think too much about that, Frank. With the war and my work. You know, I have no time.'

'But you must have some idea?'

'Not really. Why do you ask?'

'Well, it's just that I like you. I like you a lot.'

'I see. I don't really know much about you, Frank. Why don't you tell me about yourself?'

'Let's see. I come from San Francisco, California. That's on the west coast of America. We're not as formal as the guys from the east coast.'

'I see. What work do you do?'

'I was going to a technical school when I got called up. That's why I got put into signals. I want to open my own shop when the war is over.'

'That's good, Frank. You are thinking ahead.'

'Yes. That's why I asked you about your plans.' Frank put his arm around Carol's waist, and she moved in close to him. She leaned back into his chest. He turned her head towards him and kissed her lightly on the lips. This time Carol did not resist him, but she still felt something nagging at her conscience. Eventually, she pulled away from him.

'What's wrong, Carol. Is there someone else?'

'No. Not really.'

'What do you mean?'

'Well, I had a very close male friend who went away to New Guinea. He was killed there. I heard about it when his mother was notified.'

'Were you in love with this man?'

'I honestly don't know. Nothing romantic ever passed between us. We were just good friends, but I had decided to wait for him to come home before I decided anything. Now it doesn't matter, I guess.'

'No, I guess it doesn't.' Frank's voice had a finality in its tone. He reached for her and kissed her again. This time it was harder and more insistent. As he pulled away from her, he whispered, 'I love you, Carol.'

'Oh, Frank. I like you too. I like you a lot. I guess I must let go now and move on.'

'Yes, Carol, and I want you to know how much I need you in my life.'

*

Johnny and Jean were at their regular rendezvous at the South Brisbane hotel. She was now smoking with Johnny. Her sister had been disappointed about her smoking, and had told her so, but she had told Carol that everyone did it, and that she was working now and entitled to do whatever she wanted with her own money. Carol had told her that she didn't want to sound like her father, but that she wanted her to be careful with Johnny, so Jean had switched shifts permanently with Lucy, so she could have free time with Johnny away from Carol.

Jean wrapped her arms around Johnny and pulled him close to her. 'Johnny, you do love me. Don't you?' she asked.

'Sure, Baby.'

'You won't ever leave me now. Will you?'

'Don't worry, Baby. What's this all about anyway?'

'I need to know you love me, Johnny. That you want to be with me forever.'

'Sure, Baby. Don't sweat it.'

'Johnny, I haven't had my period this month.'

'Oh! I see.'

Johnny went quiet, and Jean began to worry. She released her grip on him and turned her head to engage his eyes. 'What's wrong, Johnny? You said you wanted me forever. This just makes it right for us to get married. Doesn't it, Johnny?'

'Oh sure, Baby. But don't worry just yet. These things happen sometimes for no reason. How long is it anyway?'

'I'm a few weeks overdue.'

'Oh, that's nothing to worry about. You'll probably get it anytime now.'

'Yes, I suppose so. It's just that I'm usually so regular.'

'But, Baby, it could just be because you're tired, or worried about something. These things happen. Don't worry. Just wait a bit longer, and we'll work it out then. Ok?'

'Yes, you're probably right. I'm beginning to worry too much. Like my sister.'

Johnny smiled. They got dressed and left the hotel. When Johnny got back to the signal office, he applied for a transfer to New Guinea.

*

That night, when Jean got home from work, Carol and her father were waiting for her. 'I want to speak with you, Jean,' Alan said.

'What about?' Jean asked.

'About you driving around in a Jeep with a Yank.'

'How do you know about that? Have you been spying on me again?'

'No. One of my mates saw you.'

'Well then. What about it?'

'I thought we had agreed that this would not happen.'

'Well, it has. I like Johnny, and I'm going to continue seeing him.'

'Oh, it's Johnny now, is it? I suppose you know that all Yanks are called Johnny or Joe.'

'That's his real name. Anyway, so what? I'm sick and tired of all this questioning. I'm old enough to make up my own mind.'

'You're just a girl.'

'I'm not a girl. I'm nearly seventeen, and a woman. I work for a living, and anyway, a lot of sixteen-year-olds get married and have children.'

'So, now it's marriage and children, is it?'

Carol tried to cut in. 'Wait a minute. Both of you.'

'You stay out of this. A great job you did of looking out for your sister.'

'That's not fair, Dad. I can't stop Jean from seeing boys. She's working now. In a place that's full of boys, and now that we are on different shifts, I can't look out for her,' Carol replied defensively.

'Are they boys or men? How old is this Johnny, anyway?' Alan asked, moving closer to Jean.

'Nineteen. He's just right for me,' Jean replied eagerly.

'Am I the only sane person here?' Alan paused then continued, 'What sort of future do you think you will have with this Yank? Don't you realise that even if it all works out for you, you will have to leave your family here in Australia and go with him to America?'

'I hadn't thought that far ahead, but it will be all right. I'll still come back to visit. Anyway, he might want to stay in Australia.'

'And just how do you think you will pay for all these trips back home? With some of the stardust in your eyes, I suppose,' Alan said sarcastically.

'No. I can save up for trips,' Jean replied, somewhat deflated.

Alan took a more conciliatory tack. 'Is there nothing I can say that will stop you seeing this Yank?'

'No, Dad. I love him. There, I've said it, and I'm glad I have. I love him dearly.'

Alan raised his hand as if to strike Jean, but Carol got in between them. He put his raised hand on his forehead, closed his eyes, and sighed before he turned and stormed out of the room, slamming the door behind him.

'Please be careful, Jean,' Carol said, after her father had left. 'You know that Dad is partly right. You are very young. Certainly too young for marriage.'

'Now it's you too. I suppose you want me to stop seeing Johnny as well.'

'No. I don't want you to stop seeing Johnny. He seems like a nice young man, but you do have to start seeing the long term at some point. Dad is right about your having to go away from us, and anyway, isn't there a lot you would like to do before you get married? What about saving for a trip to New Zealand. You always said you wanted to see the snow, and once you get married, you'll never be able to take a trip. All your money will go to your family.'

'Oh, Carol, I don't want to leave you here and go away, and I would like to see snow. Perhaps Johnny will take me to see some. I do love him so much. He's all I can think about right now.'

With that said, the two sisters embraced, and let their moment of sisterly compassion linger.

*

Carol and Frank had returned from taking in a movie and were sitting in the Victory Café having a late-night coffee. They spoke about the movie they had seen. *Casablanca* was a great movie they both agreed, and Carol especially liked Rick's sacrifice in the end. Suddenly, Frank looked earnestly into Carol's eyes and asked her if she was happy.

'Yes, I am, Frank. And you? Are you happy?'

'Yes. But I could be happier. If I knew you were committed to me that would make me very happy.'

'Oh. And don't you feel I am committed? We are very good friends, after all.'

'Well, I was hoping we would promise each other something more permanent than just friendship. You know I could be posted away at any time, and I would like to know that you would be waiting for me.'

Carol thought about her feelings for Frank. He was good to her. Always respectful and considerate. Apart from his insistence on a more permanent relationship, he put no pressure on her. The truth was that she liked his interest in her. She had thought long and hard about their relationship and could not see any good reason for not accepting his offer, but still something held her back.

'What did you have in mind, Frank?' she asked.

'I want to marry you, Carol.'

'That's a very big step, and anyway, I thought your government frowned on war-time marriages.'

'Yes. That's true, but they do make exceptions.'

'Wouldn't that take a long time to arrange?'

'Yes. But we could get engaged now and marry after the war.'

'I suppose we could do that.'

'Then tell me that you will become engaged to me now, and I'll get the ring tomorrow.'

'Umm … Haven't you got one already?' Carol asked, a mischievous smile crossing her face.

'I wasn't sure you would agree,' Frank replied earnestly.

'I was kidding with you Frank, but we do have a few things to sort out first, so it was prudent of you not to get one.'

'What things, Carol?'

'Things like what a marriage would involve. Where would we live? Would you want me to go back to America with you?'

'That's what I had in mind.' Frank leaned back in his seat and took a long sip of coffee. 'Don't you want to go to the States? I thought all Australian girls wanted that.'

'Not all, Frank.' Carol smiled and continued, 'What about my father and sister? What would become of them?'

'That's up to them. Surely.'

'No, Frank. I love them dearly and don't want to leave them. I know this is not what you want to hear, but there it is.'

Frank was beginning to see why Carol had been so

elusive about their future, and Carol was happy that Frank now knew how she felt about her family.

'You do love me, Carol. I can feel it.' There was a tone of desperation in Frank's voice.

'It's true, Frank, that I do have strong feelings for you, but I also love my family.'

'But the love you have for your family is not the same as the love you have for me. With me you can be intimate.'

'That's not how I see it, Frank. Maybe the love is the same, but the expression of it is different.'

'Really? I hadn't thought of it that way, so where does that leave us now?'

'I need to know that my family will be close to me wherever we live. Both my father and sister depend on me in different ways.'

'Ok. If we live in America, your family can join us there.'

'Or we could live here in Australia.'

'I suppose. But my business opportunity will be better in America. I can't offer you more than that, Carol.'

They were silent for a while, both trying to find a way out of their impasse. Finally, Carol looked up at Frank and smiled. 'Ok, Frank. I suppose you will keep your promise and let my father and sister join us in America. Let me think about it. Would that be ok?'

'You mean you will accept my engagement?'

'I'm not sure, Frank. I might, but for now let me think about it.'

Later that night, Carol was unable to sleep. She kept going over in her mind everything that had passed between her and Frank. She kept questioning herself whether she had done the right thing. There were lots of things holding her back, but there was something more; something that was stopping her from committing, but she couldn't fathom what that something was.

*

A few days later, Frank came into the Victory Café. He walked up to Carol, who was standing near Beryl, reached into his pocket, and took out a diamond ring. He went down on one knee in front of Carol and asked her to marry him. The whole café went silent, and Carol and Beryl looked surprised. This had never happened before.

After her initial surprise, Carol wondered what she could do or say. She felt like running away because she was not prepared for a decision, but now Frank had deliberately forced it on her. She was still not ready to commit, but now she felt embarrassed for both her and Frank.

She looked down at Frank, who was smiling up at her in expectation. She was caught with no way out. She had to make up her mind then and there, and she knew Frank had planned it that way. He had been good to her, and she thought he would make a good husband. She had not been proposed to before and did not know if she would be proposed to again. All these thoughts raced through her mind instantaneously.

'I … ahh … Yes, Frank. I accept.' Her words had just come out seemingly on their own accord; like she was listening to someone else make the commitment for her.

With Carol's consent, Frank rose and placed the engagement ring on her finger. He embraced her and kissed her, and the café exploded into cheering and clapping.

Beryl offered them her congratulations. Carol closed her eyes, and a slight smile crossed her face. *What have I done?* she thought. *I hope Frank and I will be happy, and that he will keep his word about bringing my family to America.*

CHAPTER 6

It took Stan and Billy a whole week to reach Port Moresby. The Kokoda Track had become one long strip of mud and slush due to the number of soldiers and native carriers who had walked it, and the soaking rain that had fallen on it. In places, Stan's and Billy's shoes got stuck in the mud, and they had to help each other out of the quagmire. They stopped at night to sleep on the side of the track, where it was more stable. They also stopped for a cup of tea and biscuits, provided by the Salvation Army officers along the way.

Eventually though, they made it through, and ended up in a field hospital in Port Moresby. Their tattered clothes were cut from their bodies, and when the nurse removed their boots and socks, skin from the soles of their feet came off as well. The skin had become glued to their socks due to the wetness in their boots, and because they had not changed their socks for weeks. After that, it was difficult for them to walk until their feet healed. Consequently, they had to take Condy's crystals (Potassium permanganate) foot baths daily, which left their feet with a purple colour. They were also ordered strict bed rest for the first week of their stay in the hospital, which they found hard to obey, especially when they wanted to go to the toilet. They were supposed to use a bottle urinal and bed pan for their toilet needs. Neither Stan nor Billy was comfortable with this, so they used to sneak out to the toilet on their own, which constantly got them into trouble with the duty sister.

They were given three hot meals a day from the hospital kitchen, along with Kaopectate powder, which stopped their diarrhoea and helped them gain some weight. They were also given penicillin for their tropical ulcers, and the nurses bathed their ulcers with antiseptic and applied non-adherent dressing. After a week, the ulcers were starting to heal. However, the healing ulcers left visible scar tissue, which marred Billy's face. For their malaria, they were given quinine, which brought it under control. They were told that their malaria would never be cured, but it could be controlled.

On entering the hospital, Stan had requested pen and paper so he could write a letter back home to his mother and notify HQ of his survival and request that his mother be informed. A few days later, a captain arrived from HQ and informed Stan that he had sent an urgent message back to Australia to inform his mother of his survival. He also thanked Stan and Billy for their heroic fighting during the withdrawal along the Kokoda Track. He said that in his opinion their bravery had not only allowed time for the reinforcement of their position by regular Australian troops, but more importantly, the fortification of Port Moresby itself, which now had developed a strong defensive position, including heavy cannon emplacements and the establishment of an air defence. It was now impossible for the current Japanese troops to take Port Moresby. Without that time, Port Moresby would have been taken and the whole eastern seaboard of Australia open for invasion by the Japanese.

The HQ captain also said that he realised that Stan and Billy's unit had come under some criticism for not having stood their ground rather than making a fighting withdrawal. He believed that had their unit done that they would have been overrun and the way would have been clear for the Japanese to take Port Moresby before reinforcements could arrive. He asked them to keep what he had said to themselves because he did not want rumours to start about a possible division of opinion in HQ.

'Don't worry, Sir. We'll keep your secret. Won't we, Billy?' Stan assured him.

'Oh yes. Don't worry, Sir.'

'How are the boys doing on the Track?' Stan asked.

'The Japs got as far as Imita Ridge. They were within sight of Port Moresby. Then they retreated. Actually, it turned into a rout, and I'm sad to say that we found evidence of cannibalism. That's how bad their supply lines had become. Oh yes, and the American Marines are doing a magnificent job on Guadalcanal in the Solomon Islands. I think we have seen a turning point in this war against Japan. We still have a long way to go, gentlemen, but I think Australia has been saved from invasion.'

With that said, the captain thanked them once again for their service, took a step back, saluted, and took his leave.

*

One evening, not long after her acceptance of Frank's proposal, Carol arrived home from work, to find Esmay waiting for her on the verandah.

'I was waiting to see you, dear. I have some wonderful news. Stan is alive, and on his way back home. The government just notified me. Apparently, there was some confusion about his death. Anyway, he's safe and sound and coming home. They say he will have to go to the hospital for a while to recuperate. That's all they said.'

Esmay said it all in a hurry, and it took some time for Carol to take it all in. 'He's alive?' Carol asked softly.

'Yes. Alive and well.'

'Well, that's wonderful news Mrs Taylor. I'm very happy for you.' Carol looked down at her engagement ring, and Esmay followed her gaze.

'Oh. You're engaged now, are you, dear?'

'Yes. It only just happened. I wish I had known about Stan. You see, I … it's just that …' Carol let her words trail off. She couldn't believe it had happened like this. Just a few days had made all the difference, and now she was left wondering what her future would be like with Stan back home because she still had strong feelings for him.

'Well, never mind, dear. I'm sure it's all for the best. These things have a way of working themselves out.'

'Yes. I expect they do. It's just that I didn't know Stan was alive when I got engaged.'

'Yes, dear, I know. Never mind that now.'

'I suppose so …' Carol wanted to say more – to tell Esmay how she felt about Stan, but she stopped short of saying anything, believing it would only cause Esmay to worry unnecessarily.

'Tell you what,' Esmay went on, 'I'm going to see Stan when he is in hospital. Would you like to come along with me?'

'Yes, Mrs Taylor. I would like that very much. Thank you.'

With that said, Esmay left, and Carol went inside.

'Who was that?' Jean asked.

'Mrs Taylor. Apparently, Stan is alive and coming home.'

A look of confusion passed over Jean's face. 'Well, that's great. Mrs Taylor will have her son back. But what about you, Carol? Do you still want Stan?'

'Yes. I do,' Carol replied, a desperate look of entrapment in her eyes.

'Well, what are you going to do?'

'I don't know, Jean. I really don't know.'

*

It was decided to send Stan and Billy back home to Australia, so within three weeks they found themselves on board the Australian hospital ship (AHS) *Wanganella* bound for Brisbane. All Australian hospital ships had large red crosses painted on their sides to hopefully allow them to pass without attack from Japanese submarines. However, news of a Japanese submarine's sinking the AHS *Centaur* reached them before they sailed, so they were all very worried that a similar fate might befall them. Due to this new danger, they were given an escort of three Australian Bathurst-class corvettes: HMAS *Deloraine*, HMAS *Katoomba* and HMAS *Lithgow*. These corvettes were Australian-built ships from the Cockatoo Island dockyard, and gave those on board the *Wanganella* some comfort, knowing the corvettes were there, and that they were crewed by Australians.

On the way to Brisbane, an incident occurred that had everyone on edge. HMAS *Deloraine* picked up a radar pattern for a submarine off her port bow. She broke formation and sped towards the signal bounce. The other two corvettes came about and laid alongside the *Wanganella*'s port side, thereby providing a shield against a possible torpedo attack.

HMAS *Deloraine* reached the spot of the signal and began laying down a pattern of depth charges, which were rolled into the sea from its stern. The large eruptions from the exploding depth charges caused the water to explode upwards in tall rushes of bubble and froth. *Kaboom! Kaboom! Kaboom!* Towards the end of its pattern, a conspicuous oil slick emerged from the ocean floor and some debris surfaced followed by two dead Japanese sailors. One of the depth charges had made a direct hit on the submarine, which had broken it apart. Although Billy was relieved that his ship had not come under attack, he felt sorry for the Japanese submariners. It was a terrible way for anyone to die.

They eventually arrived at Bretts Wharf in Brisbane, where Billy and Stan were to say their goodbyes. Stan was being transferred to the Army General Hospital in Greenslopes, while Billy was to go by train to the Heidelberg Military Hospital in Melbourne.

'Well, I guess this is goodbye, old mate,' Stan said.

'Yeah. You've been a good mate, Stan,' Billy replied. 'Couldn't have made it without you.'

'Same for me, Billy. Same for me. Look, we'll keep in touch, mate. We've been through too much together for it to end here.'

'Oh, for sure, Stan! For sure.'

They were both becoming emotional, so Stan put out his hand and they shook hands. 'Well, good luck to you, Billy. Hope to see you again someday.'

'Yes. Best of luck to you, too.' Billy's face twisted into a troubled expression as he placed his hand on his forehead. 'Good god, Stan. Do you reckon we'll ever be the same?'

Stan knew that the memories he had of his struggle on the Owen Stanley Range of New Guinea were seared into his brain forever. He carried some physical reminders of that struggle, but it was the mental wounds that would be the hardest for him to bear. As it was, Stan already had trouble sleeping. He often woke up in a cold sweat and shook from fear, his heart pounding from an adrenaline rush.

'No, Billy. I think we'll carry that bloody track with us for the rest of our lives.'

CHAPTER 7

One day after Carol returned from her shift at the Victory Café, she asked Jean, 'Mrs Cooper wants to know how long you will be away sick.'

For some time now, Carol had noticed that Jean had been acting out of sorts. When Carol first approached her about it, Jean simply said that she had not heard from Johnny for some time, so Carol had asked Frank about it. Frank told her that Johnny had been posted to New Guinea and had offered to pass on any letters that Jean wrote. Jean wrote Johnny several letters, to which he never replied.

For a while, Jean continued to come to work, but she was sad and listless, and did not engage with others in her usual way. Beryl was worried that Jean's attitude would lose her customers. Then Jean got sick and stayed away from work.

'I don't know. I feel so weak and listless. Am I really needed?' Jean replied.

'You know that Mrs Cooper likes to have you there, but not when you are like this. Have you seen a doctor?'

'Yes. He gave me some tablets.'

'Well? What's wrong with you, Jean?'

'I … ah … that is … I … I'm pregnant, Carol.'

'What? Oh my … gosh … oh my.' Carol didn't know what to say. The news was something she had not expected. She was still trying to take the news in when Jean spoke again.

'Carol, I need you to be with me on this. We'll have to tell Dad, and I don't know what he will do.'

'Yes. Yes … of course, Jean. I will support you.'

Jean sat down on the sofa and started to cry. Carol went to her and put her arm around her.

Jean looked up at Carol and mumbled, 'I know I've let you and Dad down, but this is still my child.'

At this point, Alan arrived home from work. Before entering the house, he took his boots off at the front door and placed them on the porch next to the door. 'What's going on?' he asked on entering the house. 'Why is Jean crying?'

'Dad, Jean has something to tell you. Go on, Jean, you must tell Dad now.'

'Yes. Dad, I'm pregnant. I'm carrying Johnny's child, and he has been posted overseas.'

Alan stood there taking in the news about his younger daughter. He shifted on his feet like he was preparing to run away. Then he said, 'I see. So, we can't count on him for anything, I suppose. And Carol, I thought you were looking after Jean. How did you let this happen?'

'I'm sorry ...'

'This has nothing to do with Carol, Dad. This is all my fault. I changed shifts so I could be with Johnny without Carol being there. As for Johnny, Dad, he is not answering my letters, so I guess you are right there.'

'Umm ... I don't know .... I .... I have to think,' he said, and went to his bedroom, closing the door quietly behind him.

Carol and Jean waited patiently for his return. He was gone for about half an hour before he came back out. 'Jean, you are still my daughter, and we will stand by you, love. If we don't, no one else will. Sometimes you meet the wrong kind of person, and they take advantage of you, but you can always count on your family, love. We will always be here for you.'

'Thank you, Dad. That's really what I needed to hear right now. You don't know what a relief it is for me to hear you say that, and to finally have it off my chest. I have been sick with worry, wondering how I was going to tell you.'

'You are so young, Jean. So young and innocent. I

should not have let you work. I am partly to blame for this too.'

'No, Dad. I am fully responsible, and I'm glad I'm carrying Johnny's baby, because I still love him, and I'll love his baby.'

'Yes, that's important, Jean. It's not the young'un's fault. Of course, we will love him or her as one of our own.'

The three of them came together with their arms around one another. 'Now. What's for dinner? I'm starved,' Alan said, and they went from the lounge room to the kitchen, each of them with a relieved smile on their faces.

*

Carol and Esmay caught trams from Brisbane over the Victoria Bridge and out along Logan Road to the 112th Australian General Hospital. When they alighted from the tram, they had a short, brisk walk to the hospital.

Originally, the hospital was located at Kangaroo Point, almost under the Storey Bridge and adjacent to the Evans Deakin shipyard. Although the hospital had large red crosses painted on the roof, it could have been accidently bombed by planes trying to destroy the bridge or the shipyards, so it was decided to move the hospital to Greenslopes.

The Greenslopes hospital was built on a ridge running east from Stephens Mountain. The hospital was comprised of three pavilion-style ward blocks with wide verandahs enclosed by triple-hung windows.

Carol and Esmay found Stan sitting in a large canvas chair on the verandah of the medical ward overlooking a manicured lawn that swept down to Norman Creek and a low hill covered in shrubs. The medical ward was full of patients with tropical diseases such as malaria, dengue fever and intestinal diseases.

'Hello, Stan,' Esmay said, embracing her son. 'I've brought Carol along to see you.'

Carol greeted Stan with a broad smile. 'It's good to see you again, Stan. We thought you had been killed.'

'Yes, I know,' Stan replied, returning Carol's smile. He yearned to embrace her but held back his feelings, knowing that so much had changed between them. He slowly explained the circumstances that had led to the misreporting of his death.

'Well, it's all for the best now, Stan,' Esmay said. 'We're all here now.'

'How long do you think you'll be in hospital for, Stan?' Carol asked.

'Hard to say really. Maybe a few weeks. It all depends on when my strength comes back.'

Carol wondered how she would tell Stan about Frank without affecting his recovery.

'You see, I have malaria and an unknown intestinal disease,' Stan explained.

'Oh dear,' whispered Esmay.

'Well, they're giving me quinine for the malaria and an antibiotic for my other problems.'

'How do you feel with all this medication, Stan?' Carol asked.

'I'm tired all the time, and a little sick in the stomach. I also have a fever and shaking chills that come and go, but I am getting better. I can feel my strength slowly coming back thanks to the rest and medication. I don't think I'll ever be the same though, Carol. Too much has happened to me.'

'Oh, I see,' Carol replied in a hushed tone.

'Well, I'll go out for a while and get a cuppa tea. You two stay here and chat for a while,' suggested Esmay.

After she left the room, Stan looked up at Carol and took her hands in his. He looked down at the engagement ring on her finger. 'Thanks for coming to see me, Carol. It means a lot to me.'

'Oh, that's the least I can do, Stan. I'll come regularly

now I know where you are.'

'That would be great, Carol. I see you have gotten yourself engaged.'

'Yes, it was just a few days before I heard you were coming back to us. I'm sorry, Stan. I wanted to wait for you to return home before making a decision, but I thought you were …' her voice trailed off.

'That's ok, Carol. I understand. There's something I've been wanting to say for some time now.'

Carol sensed Stan was about to say something about their relationship, and tears welled in her eyes; she didn't want to explore that now, so she stopped him by putting her hand on his shoulder and leaning in towards him. 'There's no rush, Stan,' she whispered in his ear. 'Don't say anything just yet. Let it wait until you are well again.'

'Yes. Ok then.'

They were quiet after that and stared out onto the uniquely Australian view in front of them. Carol reflected on her relationship with Stan – like how she could sit with him, and not feel pressured to say anything. Just sitting together was fine with them, and so she wondered if she had made a mistake in her decision to become engaged to Frank.

*

'Pardon me, Miss. Does a Jean Sutton live here?' An American officer was standing in Carol's doorway late one Sunday morning. She noticed the same military insignia that Frank and Johnny wore on their uniform, so Carol knew he must be from the same unit as them.

'Yes, I'm her sister. Can I help you?'

'Well, Miss. I believe that your sister is expecting Johnny Slade's child.'

'Right again, Captain.'

'Yes. Umm … We took up a collection for her, and I would like to give it to her.'

By this time, both Jean and Alan had joined Carol in the doorway. 'That's kind of you. I suppose Frank is responsible for this?' Carol asked.

'He did tell us about your sister's situation, but we all wanted to help. Maybe she can buy things for the child with the money we have collected.'

'Look, Captain,' Alan said, 'we look after our own, and we don't need any charity on your part. Where is the father anyway? Shouldn't he be here?'

'He has been posted to a combat unit overseas, Sir.'

'Why? Did you want him out of the way because he had fathered a child?'

'No, Sir. Nothing like that. In fact, he requested the posting himself. He told me he wanted to see some action. This was before I discovered the news about your daughter.'

'I see. Well, don't bother us with your conscience anymore. Good day.' Alan closed the door, and walked to the back of the house, muttering to himself about 'the nerve of some people'.

Jean slipped outside and caught the captain as he was walking to his Jeep.

'I'm sorry about my father, Captain. He can be a very proud man sometimes. I appreciate what you are trying to do for me. The truth is, I will have to stop work soon, and then I will have to rely on my father and sister for money, so I would like to take your offer, if you still want me to have it.'

'Yes, Miss Sutton. I would be happy for you to take it. It's not much, I know, but it might help a little.' The captain handed Jean a roll of American dollars.

'Thank you.'

'I wish it were more,' the captain said, looking down at his shoes. Then he raised his gaze and looked Jean in the eye. 'I really am very sorry about this, Miss.'

Jean nodded her head without replying, so the captain turned and walked away. He fired the Jeep's engine into life and pulled away, leaving Jean standing alone on the sidewalk.

*

Carol insisted that Jean tell Beryl about her pregnancy, but Jean kept putting it off, and she started wearing shifts that hid her small bump. Also, the baby was carried low in her pelvis so there was not much out front.

One day, Carol insisted that they tell Beryl together while there was a lull in customers coming into the café. Carol could tell that Jean was nervous and uncomfortable by the way she swayed on her feet when she stood in front of Beryl.

'Is there something you want?' Beryl asked, placing a hand firmly on the till and tilting her head to one side.

'Yes, Mrs Cooper … I umm … that is I …' Jean looked at Carol, and her eyes pleaded for Carol to say something on her behalf.

'What Jean wants to tell you, Mrs Cooper, is that she is expecting a child.'

'Oh, I see.' Beryl turned back to Jean and set her chin firmly. 'Well, dear, how much longer can you work for? You have been a good employee, so you can take as much time as you want.'

Jean was a bit embarrassed now because she was already six months along in her pregnancy. 'Well Mrs

Cooper, I guess I'll have to leave sometime in the next two months.'

'Well, you certainly kept that to yourself. I suppose I can get a replacement in that time. There is a wartime shortage of labour you know, so it will have to be someone young again I suppose. Do you know anyone, Jean?'

'No, Mrs Cooper, but Lucy might know someone.'

Jean had told Lucy about her predicament when they arranged to change their shifts back so that Jean could be on the same shift as Carol. Lucy had later mentioned that she might have a friend who would be interested in taking Jean's place at the café.

'Yes, well I'll ask her, but it will be hard getting someone to replace you. You are good with the customers, Jean.'

'Thank you, Mrs Cooper,' Jean said. 'And thank you for not judging me.'

'Oh, it's too late for that, dear. Anyway, I'm only interested in your work here. Anything outside is your own affair. I told your father as much when he came to see me. He must have suspected something like this would happen.'

Jean lowered her head and began to sway on her feet again. 'Yes, I suppose he did,' she said quietly.

'What is his attitude now?'

'He has accepted me and my baby.' Jean looked up and caught Beryl's stare. Their eyes held each other's until Beryl looked away.

'Well, you're lucky to have such a good father, Jean.' Beryl shifted in her seat and waved her hand to indicate that they were finished.

When they got home that night, Jean was so tired, and her feet were so sore from standing all day that she went straight to bed to take the weight off her feet. When Carol checked in on her a few minutes later, she was already fast asleep.

*

Johnny was posted to the United States 32nd Infantry Division fighting at Buna in the north-eastern part of New Guinea. Buna was in a bad location in the eastern region of a swamp formed by the delta system of the Girua River. To get there, the Americans had to force their way through a steamy jungle, which left them exhausted and demoralised.

Once again, Allied intelligence was deficient in that it told the Americans that they would face no more than 1,500 to 2,000 poorly prepared Japanese soldiers.

In truth, there were more than 6,500 Imperial Japanese Army soldiers, who were well fortified with bunkers and mutually supporting positions that created crossfire killing zones – a very difficult task for an inferior attacking force. Consequently, the American attack broke down and stalled.

Johnny found himself sending urgent messages for help and receiving messages from General MacArthur's High Command that questioned the fighting ability of the American soldiers and the leadership of their officers.

It was at this point that Johnny got sick but had to keep working because of his skill as a front-line signal sergeant. Like the Australians before them, the Americans became sick from malaria, dengue fever, bush typhus and tropical dysentery. As well as this, the tall, sharp-edged Kunai grass caused cuts that later festered into hideous tropical ulcers.

Johnny eventually contracted several of these diseases, which frequently rendered him unable to perform his duty. The standard rule for soldiers suffering from malaria was that they had to have a temperature of 105F before they could be evacuated to a field hospital. Since Johnny's temperature only ever reached 103F, he was kept in the field, unable to be hospitalised or evacuated.

General MacArthur decided to sack the American field commanders and replace them with what he believed was a more aggressive command. The new commander, however, faced the same problems as the old one, and it wasn't until the allies at Buna were reinforced with more American and Australian troops that things began to change. With better artillery and tank support, the allies were finally able to rid this New Guinea area of the Japanese menace.

Meanwhile, Johnny became more unwell with every passing day. As well as his diseases, he had developed ulcers and foot rot from walking in mud and slush and not changing his socks or boots. It became clear that he could no longer perform his duty efficiently, and so it was decided to evacuate him. However, this came too late, as his spleen ruptured one night, and he died quietly in his sleep.

*

Carol and Stan sat on the verandah, looking out on the familiar view. It had been weeks since Carol had first visited Stan. Since then, she had been to see him many times. She had also been on dates with Frank and had not told him about her feelings for Stan. She had mentioned that she was visiting Stan, but beyond that, Frank remained ignorant of the emotional turmoil that Carol was going through. She was engaged to Frank but found it hard to let go of Stan. She kept telling herself that Stan was still too sick for her to say anything about her feelings for him, but she knew that was not true, now that Stan had virtually made a full recovery.

'They kept me here longer than I thought they would,' Stan said, his voice breaking the silence of their thoughts.

'Yes,' Carol replied.

'I guess they want to be sure before they let me go.'

'I suspect so.'

'I feel fine now. It can't be much longer before they send me home,' Stan said, smiling at Carol.

'Yes. That's something to look forward to. Coming home to your mother.'

'Umm ... Carol, there is something I need to tell you. Something I've been meaning to say ever since I got back. I've been going over it in my mind so many times, and I think now is the right time to tell you.'

Carol began to panic. She knew that Stan would say something personal about them, and that this would force her to confront what she had been desperately trying to avoid. 'Yes, Stan. I have something to say to you too,' Carol replied, with a nervous strain in her voice.

This caused Stan to concentrate. He frowned and lines furrowed the small patch between his eyebrows. 'What is it, Carol?'

'Well Stan, as you know, I am engaged to an American soldier.' She stopped and her eyes pleaded with Stan for his understanding.

'Yes, I know, and that's fine, Carol. I'm sure he is a great bloke. If you love him, he must be.'

'But I love you too, Stan,' Carol blurted out. She was unable to stop herself from telling Stan how she felt about him, and now she felt embarrassed by her forthrightness. *Gosh*, she thought. *That just came out so fast that I had no time to think about what I was saying.*

'I love you too, Carol. We will always be the best of friends. That's what you wanted to say. Isn't it?'

Carol felt moisture welling in her eyes. It would be so easy for her to just let Stan go right now, but still she wanted to know how he really felt about her. 'I guess so, Stan. But I do have strong feelings for both of you. With you I can relax and be myself, and with Frank it is something different.'

What she meant, but could not tell Stan, was that although it had been a slow start with Frank, Frank was more emotional than Stan, more intense. She reasoned, however, that seeing Stan in a hospital was not very romantic; but then again, Stan had never made an advance on her. In the whole time she had come to see him, he had just made small talk and sat quietly with her. It was true that she had not wanted him to say anything that would cause her to confront what she was now facing, but she wished he had said something – given her some indication of how he felt about her. Instead, she had been left to wonder if he loved her too. Still, Stan exhibited a quiet strength that drew Carol closer to him. She thought, *He may not be as passionate as some, but he is dependable.* Ultimately, Carol felt safe and comfortable in Stan's presence, and she also found that incredibly attractive.

'How do you mean, Carol? How is it different?'

'I don't know, Stan. It just is.'

'I guess you have made up your mind. After all, you are engaged to him. Right?'

'No. My mind is not really settled, Stan. You see, I thought you were dead when I got engaged. Then I learnt that you were here. It's been very difficult for me, Stan. I am so confused about all this. I think about it all the time. It keeps going round and round in my mind. I feel guilty whichever way I turn, and I can't seem to get any resolution. I just keep drifting and hoping that it will work itself out, but it never does.'

Falling into his arms, Carol broke down and started to cry. She placed her head on his chest and sobbed. 'Can't you just tell me that you love me and want to be with me – not just as friends?'

'Carol, I do love you. I have loved you for a long time now. It was the thought of coming back to you that kept me alive in New Guinea, but I am changed. The war has changed me. I am not the person you knew before I went away.'

'How have you changed, Stan?' Carol asked, sitting up and looking at him quizzically.

'It's hard to say, and I really don't want to talk about it, but for one thing I have disturbed sleep now. I have seen and done horrible things, Carol. Things that no one should see or do. So, I don't think I am a good prospect as a husband anymore. If you married me, you would have to be as much a nurse as a wife, and I really don't want that for you. I love you too much for that. I think it would be better if you married your American fiancée. I think that would be the best for both of us.' Stan said it with such conviction that Carol lowered her head. She brought his hands up to her lips and kissed them.

'Oh, Stan. You are a good man. I wish our

circumstances were different … and I wouldn't mind being your nurse.'

'Let's not complicate it anymore, Carol. We will always be the very best of friends.'

They drifted back into silence before Carol left for the tram that would carry her home.

Sitting alone on the verandah after Carol had left, Stan felt like he was falling into a deep, dark hole. He tried to catch himself, but the truth was that he still wanted Carol even though he knew he would never have her. Not now. An immeasurable ache filled his chest. He covered his face with his hands. *What else could I have said?* Stan loved Carol too much to be a burden on her, and he didn't want to stand in the way of her chance at happiness.

*

It was a mild June morning. The sky was clear, and the morning sun soaked into Jean's body as she sat in a cane chair on her front verandah. Both Carol and her father were at work and Jean had taken the opportunity to sleep in. She was still in her dressing-gown and her hair had not been combed. Jean had given up her work at the Victory Café because she was now in the final stage of her third trimester; her feet had swollen, so it was hard to stand all day.

She sat in the sun enjoying the splendour of the moment, with her feet raised on an empty fruit carton that her father had got for her from his work. She was content with her situation, despite how others might feel about an unmarried mother. She loved the prospect of bearing Johnny's child and looked forward to the coming birth. She had continued writing to Johnny, despite not having received any response. In her heart, she hoped he would one day return to her and their child.

As she sat going over in her mind past events with Johnny and wondering where he was now, a Jeep pulled up outside her home, and the same captain who had previously come to her with money alighted and walked to her gate. 'Good morning, Miss Sutton. May I come in?'

Jean was embarrassed by her looks; her hand went to her hair as she tried to straighten it out. 'Yes. Of course, Captain. What is it you want?'

As the captain entered the yard and walked up to Jean, she tried to stand. 'Please don't get up, Miss. I have some bad news for you, and it's better that you remain seated.'

Jean sat back down. 'What is it? Is it something about Johnny?'

'Yes, Miss. How much do you know about him?'

'I know that I love him, and that I am carrying his child, and that I hope he comes back to us after the war.'

'Yes. Well … like I said, I have some bad news for you. I am sorry, Miss, but Johnny died in the service of his country. He got very sick and died a few weeks ago.'

'Oh, I see.' Tears immediately sprang to Jean's eyes, and she started sobbing uncontrollably. The captain knelt beside her and embraced her, letting her hold him tightly. Eventually, Jean stopped crying and broke her embrace; then she wiped her nose with the back of her hand. The captain gave her his handkerchief, which she used to clean her face. 'Thank you for coming and giving me this news, Captain. I am grateful to you.'

The captain stood back up before replying. 'Yes, Miss. I guess you didn't know that Johnny was an orphan?'

'No, I didn't. He didn't talk about himself very much.'

'Well, he was, and he made out his GI life insurance to you and the child.'

'Oh. What's that?'

'May I sit down?'

'Yes, of course Captain. I'm sorry I didn't offer before.

Please sit.' Jean waved her hand at the chair next to her, and the captain sat down.

'All American soldiers are able to insure themselves for five dollars a month,' he continued. 'Johnny took out that policy when he started dating you. It is worth ten thousand US dollars, and Johnny wanted that money to go to you and his child.'

'Does that mean I will get ten thousand dollars?'

'Unfortunately, Miss, the government insists that the money must go to a 'next of kin', and since you were not married to Johnny, you are not eligible. The government insists on that because they do not want GIs to sign over their payment to just anyone they happen to meet overseas.'

'Oh, I see. I guess that makes sense.' Jean paused for a moment, then went on, 'Well, it's still nice to know that Johnny was thinking of me and our baby. Thank you for coming to tell me, Captain.'

"Yes, Miss. But I don't think we should leave it at that. You see, in his last will and testament, Johnny insisted that he is the father of your child. I have read the attached letter to his will, and he states that he does not want his child to grow up thinking that his father deserted him. I guess he must have had second thoughts about what he had done to you.'

'Well, that is nice to know too. I always thought that Johnny loved me and would return to us.'

There was a moment when they both sat quietly on the verandah.

'You know, Miss Sutton,' the captain finally said, 'before the war I was a lawyer. I could represent you in making a legal claim on behalf of you and your child. You see, I believe that your child has a legal right to claim that he or she is Johnny's child and an American citizen, and would, therefore, be entitled to the insurance payment.'

'Really? Well, what would that entail?'

'You would have to provide me with a retainer to be your representative, and then I could start the legal procedures.'

'Oh, that's very kind of you to offer, Captain, but I don't have much money. I don't think I could afford that.'

'Don't worry about that, Miss Sutton … may I know your first name? It seems strange calling you Miss all the time.'

Jean smiled and nodded. 'Jean. My first name's Jean. And yours?'

'Benjamin Levi. That's my name. But please call me Ben. I will take whatever you can afford right now, Jean, and that will be the full and final payment. We lawyers sometimes work on a pro-bono basis, and I would like to take on your case under those conditions.'

'That's very kind of you, Ben.' Jean opened her purse and took out a ten-shilling note. 'Will this be enough?' she asked.

'Oh, that's too much, Jean. Just give me a silver coin.'

Jean produced a florin, and Benjamin took it. Then, he opened his briefcase and took out some papers. He wrote the amount Jean had given him on a set of documents. Next, he signed them and handed them to Jean.

'These are the papers giving me the right to represent you in this matter.' He indicated where Jean was to sign, and she obliged. When it was all over Jean spoke up.

'May I ask why you want to help me, Ben?'

'Johnny was a member of my unit, so I feel some responsibility for the events that have happened. Also, I have a great deal of sympathy for your situation. I want to do all I can for you and your child.'

'That's very good of you.' Jean offered Ben her hand, which he took and shook. 'Well, thank you once again for all that you are doing for me and my baby.'

'That's fine, Jean. Oh yes … It may take some time to finalise all this, but don't worry, I'll keep in touch with you as your case progresses. The US government can be very slow with these things, but I promise I will do all that I can to speed it up.'

'Yes, I can imagine that it will take time.'

'One other thing, the government might require a blood test to be done on the baby. I hope that won't be a problem.'

'No. If they need it, I'll get it done at the hospital.'

'Well, that's all for now. Please don't get up. I'll see myself off.' With that said, Ben rose and looked down at Jean. 'I'm very sorry for all that has happened to you, Jean, and I'll do my best to get that money for you and your baby.'

'Thank you, Ben. I am very grateful for what you are doing for us.'

Captain Levi left quietly. Jean tilted her head slightly to one side as tears, once again, started to well in her eyes.

CHAPTER 8

For some time now, Stan had been working in the government Lands Office in Adelaide Street. After he had been discharged from hospital, he was ruled unfit for military service and was discharged from the army. The government had felt honour bound to offer Stan a clerical position in its bureaucracy. His work consisted mainly of filing deeds to property, which was not too taxing on his physical capacity. He finished work at 5 pm and had fallen into the habit of going to the Victory Café to wait for Carol to finish her shift, then escorting her home.

One hot November day, with American and Australian soldiers on leave passes drinking in the pubs and bars around town, Stan and Carol set off from Queen Street, passing the AMP building housing MacArthur's HQ, and turning into Creek Street on their way home. Up ahead of them, outside the American PX, they saw three Australian soldiers approach an American signalman. Carol said she recognised the insignia on the American's uniform.

'That's a soldier from Frank's unit,' she said. 'I saw him at a dance once.'

'Oh! I wonder what the Australians want.'

When Stan and Carol reached the Gresham Hotel on the corner of Creek and Adelaide streets, they saw two American MPs approach the soldiers, and ask to see the American's leave pass. Once he began to fumble through his pockets in a vain attempt to find it, the MPs became impatient, and began roughing him up.

'Look at that, Stan. Those American MPs are manhandling that poor soldier. They are so quick to use physical force, and they like to use their batons too. I hope they don't start using them now.' *They also have guns,* Carol thought, *and I have never seen so many guns on our streets. I wonder why Americans love their guns so much?*

Stan stopped walking and watched the spectacle unfolding on the opposite side of the road. The Australian soldiers told the MPs to stop badgering 'their mate'. Although the MPs had no jurisdiction over the Australians, they began to beat the Australians with their batons.

Stan was disgusted by this brutal display of force on his countrymen, so he rushed over to help them. He caught one of the MPs by surprise with a rugby tackle, burying his shoulder into the MP's midriff, and knocking the wind out of him. They both went down hard on the pavement with Stan on top. The MP lay there trying to get his wind back.

Stan got up and turned his attention to the other MP. He began throwing punches at his head and the MP responded by using his baton on Stan, who raised his arms to avoid being hit in the head. This meant the American MP was now under siege from the three Australian soldiers and Stan. Soon the other MP regained his feet and came up behind Stan. He swung his baton hard and cracked Stan on his knee. Pain shot through Stan's body and made him drop to one knee while the MP began beating him all over his body. Stan lay down on the pavement and covered his head once again. Before long, both MPs directed their attention back to the three Australian soldiers, beating them mercilessly with their batons.

By this time, several other Australian soldiers and citizens rushed in to save their fellow countrymen from a terrible beating. As the crowd surged forward, the American signalman, who had originally been asked for his leave pass, retreated to the safety of the American PX, and was followed by the MPs.

Meanwhile, Stan was being trampled underfoot by the ever-growing crowd, so Carol rushed over and stood over him. She pleaded for someone to help her get him out of harm's way. Eventually, she was able to get Stan to his feet and help him to the other side of the road. Stan's knee was now blowing up and turning blue, and he could not put any weight on it, so they stayed on the opposite side of the road to watch what would happen next.

By this stage the Australian crowd had become quite large and vocal. More MPs arrived, whistles were being blown and the MPs formed a makeshift cordon around the entrance to the PX. Somebody from the crowd threw a bottle, which was followed by more bottles and whatever the crowd could gather. Eventually, a parking sign was unearthed from its position and hurled through the front window of the PX. Alarm bells began ringing loudly, and the MPs flayed into the crowd with their batons. The crowd surged forward and broke the cordon. Entering the ground floor of the PX, the crowd carried out widespread looting and destruction.

The 738th MP Battalion arrived, armed with 12-guage shotguns, and turned their weapons on the crowd. This led to one death and several injuries to the Australian mob, who, in turn, became further enraged. Australian soldiers arrived with weapons and the Battle of Brisbane began.

An ambulance arrived and Stan, accompanied by Carol, was taken to the General Hospital for treatment. The waiting room that Stan was taken to smelled of chlorine and baking-soda-based cleaning fluids, and the floors were highly polished. Laminated tiles ran from the floor to hip high on the walls.

A sister took one look at Stan's knee and sent him into the triage section of the ward. Stan and Carol waited there for about an hour before a doctor came to see him. During that time, Stan told Carol to leave him and go home.

'I'm fine, Stan. I'll wait with you. I don't want to leave you while you are in pain.'

'But it could be a long wait, Carol.'

'It's not a problem, Stan. Really.'

'What about Frank? Were you going to meet him later tonight?'

'No. And it's got nothing to do with Frank. I'm just here with an old friend.'

'Well, your old friend is feeling quite silly now. After what happened, I guess you feel I should have minded my own business.'

'No, I don't. I think you went into that ruckus in support of your fellow countrymen, and the fact that they were Australian soldiers being bashed with batons made it worse for you. I know I was upset seeing it too.'

Stan took Carol's hands and engaged her eyes. 'Yes, Carol. That's exactly how I felt, but what scares me is that the anger in me took over. I had no control over it. I seem to have a flash point now with little room for tolerance. My flash point is much lower than before. I wish I had more control.'

'That is a problem, and you will have to work on it. The fact that you recognise it is already half the battle. We can just watch out for it in future.'

'You said, *we*. What do you mean by *we*?'

'Actually, we see a lot of each other, so we can both be on the lookout for those things that strike a nerve with you. I'll tell you if I see it coming. Would that suit you, Stan? If I told you?'

'Yes, that would be great. That way I think I'll be able to calm down, if you point it out to me.'

'Good. Let's work on it together.'

Just then a doctor came in and examined Stan. The doctor ordered an x-ray of Stan's knee and provided him with two aspirin for his pain. The aspirin did little to relieve the dull ache deep within Stan's knee.

The ward began filling up with many casualties from the riots that had now broken out all over Brisbane, as American and Australian servicemen went looking for each other to beat up. Again, Stan told Carol to go home, and again she refused.

After the x-ray, Stan was returned to the ward and waited for another hour before the doctor came back to see him. 'You are lucky,' the doctor said. 'You have no broken bones, just a torn ligament and some bruising and swelling. We'll put it in a cast for you, to stop the movement. Come back in four weeks and we will remove the cast and wrap it firmly with crepe bandages. You should be able to give it light exercise by then. If you feel any pain, you must stop and relax your knee. It will never heal if you don't stop and give it time to heal. You can also take up to six aspirin a day for the pain, but the pain should be over in a day or two.'

The doctor disappeared again, and a wardsman came and took Stan to the section where casts were made. By this time the swelling had stopped; it took about twenty minutes to apply the cast, and a further thirty minutes for the cast to dry, which ran from Stan's foot all the way up to his thigh. Stan was given a pair of crutches and told to come back in four weeks to have the cast removed. He was also warned to watch his toes; if they went blue at any time, he was to come back to the ward immediately to have the cast removed.

When Carol returned home that night, Jean told her that Frank had called to see her. He had waited for over an hour before he left and had seemed upset at not having seen her.

*

There were riots on the streets of Brisbane for two days after the incident, which had resulted in many being taken to hospital. Australian and American soldiers stalked each other, sometimes with loaded weapons in their hands. Sporadic fighting broke out all over the Brisbane CBD. These two days were notoriously referred to as 'The Battle of Brisbane'.

Women were escorted through Brisbane by soldiers with fixed bayonets. Carol would walk to Central Station and join a group with other women, and they were then flanked by the soldiers who accompanied them to their work. At the close of her shift, soldiers were waiting to take her back. On one of these nights, however, Frank was there to meet her. 'Hi Carol, I must deliver some equipment to the CO on Mount Coot-tha. Do you feel like coming for a drive?'

'Oh sure,' Carol replied. 'Just let me get my things.' Carol hurried to the back of the room and returned wearing a sweater.

They drove through Brisbane, Auchenflower, and the outlying suburbs of Brisbane in silence. Carol thought there was something on Frank's mind, so she waited for him to open the conversation, and when he didn't, she felt awkward. She pulled her sweater close to her chest and wrapped her arms around herself.

'These Jeeps can be very cold,' Frank said.

'I'm not that cold really. Don't worry about me.' They drifted into silence once again. Carol enjoyed the view of Brisbane as the Jeep climbed the mountain.

Carol explained that Mount Coot-tha had been the home of the Turrbal Aboriginal people, who used to collect the local honey that they called 'Ku-Ta', hence the name of the mountain. 'Mount Coot-tha is the highest peak in Brisbane. It forms the western edge of the Taylor Range, which runs for approximately four miles from the Brisbane CBD.'

Anti-aircraft guns and searchlights were located on the lookout, which was fenced off so that civilians could not enter. It was to this unit that Frank was now delivering the equipment. When they arrived at the gate of the unit, Frank turned the Jeep around, so it pointed back down the mountain. He left the Jeep in gear and applied the handbrake. He also took a rock and placed it under the front wheel, saying to Carol, 'You can't be too careful with these Jeeps.'

'Oh, yes,' agreed Carol.

'You can't come in here. Do you mind waiting? I won't be long.'

'That's not a problem. I'll still be here when you get back.' Carol laughed at her own little joke. *Where would I go?*

'Yes. I'll see you soon,' Frank said.

For the first time since the start of their ride, Carol relaxed a little, but she was still very confused about her feelings. *Could it be possible that I love two men at the same time?* Frank was lively to be with, and always did things she enjoyed. Like this trip tonight. He was always springing these little surprises on her. Stan, on the other hand, had always been very protective, and had made her feel safe. She always felt that she didn't have to worry about anything when she was with Stan, and now she felt a strong urge to support him as well. She wondered what they would both think about her, if they knew what she was thinking. She looked out over the browned-out city lights of Brisbane. *From up here it's beautiful, and difficult to appreciate what the city has been through with the recent unrest.*

Frank returned and fired the Jeep into life. They

started back down the mountain. After a short distance, Frank drove the Jeep into a parking bay that afforded a splendid view of the city. He pulled up and applied the handbrake. When he turned the engine off and took his foot from the brake, the Jeep crept forward; the steepness of the slope was too much for the handbrake alone. Frank engaged the gearbox in reverse and that prevented the Jeep from creeping forward. He then turned to face Carol. 'Is something troubling you, Carol? We don't seem to be as close as we were,' he said.

'Oh,' Carol replied, a shot of fear running through her. 'I guess there is, Frank.' She explained about Stan's return.

'What does that mean for us?' Frank asked.

'Actually, Stan is only a close friend. We are not lovers or anything like that.'

'I certainly hope not!' Frank exclaimed sarcastically, leaning back in his seat. 'Tell me, Carol, do you still want to be my fiancée?'

There was that hesitation that always went through Carol's mind whenever she thought about her relationship with Stan. 'Yes, Frank. Why do you ask?'

'I'm just trying to understand what is going on. What were you doing with Stan for so long the other night?'

'You know he was injured, right? So, I went to the hospital with him.'

'Did you have to stay with him all night?'

Carol was beginning to resent Frank's questioning of her integrity, but at the same time she recognised that she was not being completely honest with him, *so did that give him the right to be so openly jealous?* she wondered.

'I wasn't gone all night, Frank, and Stan needed an x-ray, so it took a lot of time. Stan always stood up for me when we were growing up. I guess it just seemed the natural thing to do. To stay with him at the hospital, I mean.'

Thinking back to that night, she recalled that Stan had told her to leave him and go home. He had said Frank might not be very understanding, if he found out. Carol's mind began to race, trying to find something to say that might change the subject. 'Isn't it beautiful up here?' she offered.

'I suppose,' Frank replied. They slipped into silence.

Carol sensed he was holding back his anger. 'You know Stan was seriously injured that night.'

'You mean that night when those Australians assaulted our MPs and broke into our PX?'

He said it with venom in his voice, and Carol was immediately alerted to the change in Frank's inflection.

'I was there, Frank, and the MPs made the first move with their batons. Australians don't like that sort of thing.'

'As I understand it, those MPs were doing their job. Just trying to keep order.'

'Oh no. It was more than that – it was the use of excessive force. They didn't have to use their batons on those boys.'

'Well, I guess that's a difference of opinion we'll have to live with.'

'If you want it that way, Frank. You know I want you in my life. You know that, right?'

'Sure. I guess so. It's just that I don't want you going out with Stan.'

Carol took some time to gather her thoughts before replying, 'I'm sorry about what happened that night.' *There it was again.* She was having to apologise for something she did not want to give up. She wanted to go on seeing both Stan and Frank – she was unable to make a final break with either of them.

Frank began hitting his fist on the steering wheel, which shook with every blow. Carol recognised that she had apologised but had not said that she would stop seeing Stan, and she believed this was what angered Frank.

Suddenly, he pushed the starter button on the dashboard and engaged the gearbox. To do this he had to have one foot on the brake and accelerator, and the other on the clutch. Unfortunately, in his anger and his haste, he engaged first gear instead of reverse. The Jeep shot forward and went over the edge of the parking bay. It bumped its way down the slope, bouncing violently from side to side, as it careered over the rough terrain. Carol was thrown clear of the vehicle and broke her arm when she raised it to take the force of her collision against a large boulder. Nevertheless, her head hit the boulder and she was concussed. She slid down to the ground and lay motionless.

Meanwhile, Frank stayed with the Jeep, trying his best to steer it clear of large objects. However, the Jeep was brought to a halt when it hit a large tree. Frank was thrown out of the Jeep but was soon back on his feet. He turned and raced back to Carol.

CHAPTER 9

After saying goodbye to Stan at the Brisbane dock, Billy had been taken by army truck to South Brisbane Station, where a troop train took him to Sydney. The troop train was overcrowded and during the night soldiers slept on the floors or wherever they could stretch out. Most, however, had a sleepless night sitting up. When they reached Sydney, Billy changed trains, which took him to Albury where he again changed trains. This train took him on to Melbourne. Again, his journey was a tiring one as he bounced around on his seat with only dozes between long periods of staying awake.

It was necessary for Billy to make these train changes because of the different railway gauge in each of the different Australian states. The difference in the railway gauges was a result of the rivalry that existed before Federation between the three colonial governments, each trying to limit the import of goods from one another. If ever there was a good example of the need for a national government, this surely was it.

At journey's end, Billy found himself in the surgical ward of the 115th Heidelberg Military Hospital in West Heidelberg, which was established in March of 1941 to care specifically for wounded soldiers like Billy; and Billy was also lucky to have his case taken up by a young surgeon with an interest in the newly emerging field of cosmetic surgery. When the Japanese soldier had bitten a chunk out of Billy's cheek, it had left prominent scar tissue, which marred his face.

The young surgeon took on Billy's case and undertook a novel operation for its time. He cut the scar tissue out, then applied deep stitches to the open wound, which half closed the wound and would help in the deep healing of the cut. After that, he applied surface stitches to close the wound completely. The subcutaneous stitches would dissolve over time, and the surface stitches were removed after two weeks.

Billy was left with a slight scar on the high point of his left cheek, which gave him a strong, manly look.

Although Billy had been well cared for regarding his physical health, he carried deeper problems concerning his emotional stability. At night, he would wake up in a cold sweat to find himself wringing wet, his heart racing and his body shaking uncontrollably. He suffered flashbacks to the times he felt his life was in danger – to times when he had to kill or be killed.

He also went through times of deep depression, when he would want to stay in bed all day. At these times, the nursing team would insist that he get up and take a walk around the grounds. Whenever he did this, it helped for a time, but he was soon back to the same mood he had been in before the walk.

Billy would often sit in a cane chair looking out over a clean open area of lawn surrounded by well-manicured trees and shrubs. His mind would drift into scenes from his life; the good times with his family and mates, and the young women he had met, but wherever he started, he always ended up in the jungle of New Guinea, with thoughts of the slaughter that had taken place there – thoughts that were so close and so personal, that they seemed to rise in his mind and hang there like a morning mist that would not go away. No morning sunrise emerged in his mind to burn away the mist, so it developed into a dark, heavy fog, from which the hate-filled faces of Japanese soldiers emerged, with their long rifles and long bayonets held at the ready to thrust and stab at Billy's chest. Suddenly, they dropped – their bullet-torn bodies falling in front of Billy, piling up higher and higher, growing bigger and bigger by the hundreds. Billy's heart raced and pumped hard, his hands shook, and he sweated profusely. He would moan and shake his head, and usually ended up sitting alone on the verandah in his cane chair, looking out over the beautiful grounds that did not register in his mind, while tears rolled down his cheeks and over his chin. The horror of what he had experienced in the war was all that he could see.

As a result of these episodes, he was placed in the care of a resident psychiatrist, who tried to break through the pain and lay waste to the lingering hurt and suffering, but nothing he tried seemed to work. Psychiatrists were only just beginning to understand the effects that war could have on the mind, and it would take them some time to realise that the war-damaged minds of veterans was not the same type of troubled minds that they usually worked with.

Billy's psychiatrist decided to give him a dose of sodium amytal, which put him into a deep sleep for forty-eight hours. On waking, Billy was told to take a long hot bath, eat a hot meal, and put on fresh, clean pyjamas. After that, Billy was taken for a session with his psychiatrist, who explained to him that he was suffering from a severe case of battle fatigue, which had led to his depression. He was told that his symptoms would probably persist throughout the rest of his life, and that the only treatment for it was medication, which would help him sleep and relieve the depression, but would leave him with a tired, washed-out feeling for up to twenty-four hours after waking. He was told that he would have to try and relax as much as he could and seek out those periods in his life that could take his mind away from the killing and death he had witnessed and in which he had participated.

Billy's depression turned out to be treatment resistant. The psychiatrist tried various drugs available at the time, but they had little effect. Billy's depression persisted, and he grew tired of trying so many different drugs, and the after-effects they created. In desperation, Billy's psychiatrist turned to group sessions with others who had faced similar problems, but again, the relief it offered was only temporary, and Billy slipped back into his depression. Those treating Billy had almost given up when Billy received a letter from Stan, who had kept in touch with Billy and had followed his diagnoses and failing treatment. Stan now suggested that Billy come up to Brisbane and stay with him for a while, where he could get plenty of rest and understanding.

This news cheered Billy up. He told his carers that he wanted to go to Brisbane and be with Stan because they had been good mates in New Guinea. Billy's psychiatrist saw this as a potential breakthrough, so he arranged with a colleague at the Greenslopes hospital in Brisbane to take on Billy's case while Billy was up there. Billy promised to visit the Greenslopes psychiatrist on arrival and continue seeing him when needed.

*

Carol had been unconscious for thirty-six hours, and the doctors were very worried about her slipping into a deep coma. From the time that Jean had told Stan what had happened, they had sat beside her bed, Stan with his cast leg stuck out straight in front of him, and Jean holding Carol's free hand while stroking her arm. Stan spent hours talking to Carol about their school days together, and the quiet times they had enjoyed. Jean spoke about the light-hearted incidents they had shared as sisters, such as the time they had worn ridiculously large hats to the local baths. They had laughed together at the odd looks they had received from the other bathers.

At one time, Frank had called in to see Carol, but he did not stay long. Neither Jean nor Stan gave up their positions beside Carol, and this had left Frank standing awkwardly at the end of Carol's bed.

Stan reasoned that Frank had left because he

did not see the point in staying until Carol regained consciousness, although Stan also thought that Frank might be feeling guilty about the accident. Jean did not bother to move and let Frank sit beside Carol. Stan used the excuse for not moving that it would have been difficult for him with his leg in a cast.

On the night of the accident, Frank had reached Carol's side only to find her unconscious, and with an obviously broken arm; it stuck out from below the elbow at a grotesque angle. Realising he should not move her in case of spinal injury, he had climbed the embankment to the road, and raced back to the Mount Coot-tha unit for help. From there, a medical team was called up from Brisbane to transport Carol. The medics were careful not to bend or twist her spine when they raised her and then lowered her onto a stretcher. Frank went with her in the back of the ambulance.

When they reached Brisbane General Hospital, she was examined by several doctors, and x-rayed for other breaks to her body. With no other breaks being found, she was sent to the intensive care ward where she was to stay until she woke up or was transferred to a medical ward.

*

Billy's train arrived at South Brisbane Station early in the morning. Stan was waiting for him on the platform, which was covered in ferns hanging from baskets attached to the cast-iron balustrades holding up the platform roof, and palms in pots sat along the walls of the station. The overall effect was one of pleasing tropical greenery to greet the weary train travellers.

Stan and Billy were both delighted to see one another and shook hands enthusiastically. 'It's good to see you, mate,' Stan said.

'Yeah. I should've come up earlier, but I had a few problems.'

'Yes … Well, you're here now, and that's the main thing.' They slipped into a conversation about how good Billy's cheek looked and how Stan had got his leg in plaster. Soon all the immediate news was covered, and Stan said, 'Well, we better get you home.'

'Stan has told me so much about you, Billy,' Stan's mother said, meeting the boys at the door. 'We have set up a room next to Stan's for you.' The three of them went into Billy's room while he put his bags down against a clear part of the bedroom wall.

'Do you boys feel like a cuppa?' Mrs Taylor asked.

'Love one, Mum. What about you, Billy?'

'Yes. For sure, Mrs Taylor. Thank you.'

Stan and Billy sat at the kitchen table while Esmay prepared the Bushells Blue Label Black Tea and set out a few Gingernut biscuits on a plate.

'What did you want to do while you are here, Billy?' Stan asked.

'Well, I thought you might show me around after your cast comes off. In the meantime, we can just relax. What do you think?'

'For sure, mate. After all, you did come up here to relax.' They slipped into a brief silence.

'Why don't you and Billy take Jean on a night out, Stan?' Esmay suggested, breaking the silence. 'Maybe Carol will regain consciousness soon and the four of you could go out together.'

This opened a conversation about who Carol and Jean were. When Billy was fully briefed, he was keen to meet Jean. He felt she had been through a hard time, and that gave him a sense of kinship. They drifted in and out of silence as they sipped their tea. Stan did not feel the need to keep Billy occupied with talk; they were comfortable in each other's company. Billy showed an interest in Stan's description of the 'Battle of Brisbane' because news of it had not reached Melbourne due to wartime censorship.

'Those Yank MPs are pretty quick to use their batons, mate,' Stan said.

'I'll remember that if ever I'm out at night,' Billy replied.

*

Carol awoke to the relief of Stan, Billy and Jean, who had been watching over her that evening. Carol's doctor was called and arrived shortly after Carol began to make sense of the fact that she was in a hospital. 'What happened?' Carol asked.

'You were involved in an accident on Mount Coot-tha Road. Do you remember any of that?' the doctor asked.

'Oh, yes. That's right. Where's Frank? He was with me.'

'He's fine,' Jean offered. 'Don't worry about him.'

'You are a very lucky young lady,' the doctor continued. 'You broke your left arm protecting your head when you were thrown out of the Jeep. If you had not done that, your skull would have been crushed. As it is, you have no depression fracture, and now that you have regained consciousness, you should recover. We will have to keep you here for two more days under observation, however.'

'When can I go back to work?'

'Don't forget you have a broken arm, and we need to monitor your blood pressure,' the doctor went on. 'We also need to check that you do not bleed from your ears or nose and watch that you do not start vomiting. Once you leave us you will need to keep monitoring these things for yourself.'

'Yes, I see, Doctor, but I feel fine really. Just a little light-headed.'

'Well, that's good. I'll come back and check in on you later.'

The doctor left the room. Jean gave Carol a hug and kissed her on the cheek. 'Welcome back, sis.' She whispered into Carol's ear. 'Don't worry about work. We'll have Dad's wages, so we should be ok. We've managed on just his wages before.'

Carol smiled up at Jean. 'Thank you, Jean. I'm sorry that I have put us in this position, but I guess we don't have any other choice,' she said.

'Never mind, sis. Really. Don't worry about it.'

CHAPTER 10

Carol came out of the hospital two days later, and Frank was there with his Jeep to drive her home. 'I'm terribly sorry about what happened,' Frank said, putting Carol's things into the back of the Jeep.

'It wasn't your fault, Frank, and you did all you could to get me to the hospital. I'm grateful to you for that.' Carol got in beside Frank and he started the Jeep and drove off.

They drove in silence for a while then Frank added, 'It's just that I feel like a fool for putting the Jeep into first gear instead of reverse. I really can't understand how that could have happened.'

'Try not to worry so much about it, Frank. It could happen to anyone.'

'Yes. But it happened to me, and things like that don't usually happen to me.'

'Umm ...' Carol let the conversation hang, not wanting to go on.

'It's just that I was angered by what we had said to each

other just before it happened. I lost my concentration, you see.'

'Umm …'

Frank pulled the Jeep into the curb outside Carol's house and cut the engine. He left it in gear with the handbrake on. Then, he turned towards Carol. 'Yes, we had a difference of opinion as I recall,' he said.

'That's right … and you got a little carried away,' Carol added, and gave a little laugh. 'And how do you feel now, Frank? Now that you have had time to think about it.'

'I don't think it matters much anymore. For a while there I thought I might lose you, and that thought made everything else not very important at all. You see, I love you, Carol, and I want to marry you and take you home to America with me. Do you still want me, Carol? Do you still love me?'

'Well, lying in bed for the last two days gave me plenty of time to think, and I must say that the thought of leaving my sister and father and friends here, while I go to America, does not seem as bright a prospect as it once did.'

'So, you don't love me now. Is that it, Carol?'

'I didn't say that, Frank. It's just that I didn't realise how much I will miss Jean if I go away. I love her too.'

'Yes, but in a sisterly way, right? With me it must be different, surely.'

'I don't know about that. Like I told you before, I feel my love is all one thing, and it just flows out from me to all those I love. I know I will miss you, if you go away, and I will miss my sister, if I go away.'

They sat in silence for a while, both taking in what each had said. Then Frank got out of the Jeep. 'Let's get you inside,' he said. He came around to Carol's side and helped her out of the Jeep. Then he took her bags out of the back and led Carol inside the house. 'When do you want me to call again?' Frank asked.

Funny that Frank should ask that, Carol thought. *He usually just tells me when he is going to meet me.* She wondered if she had offended him by what she had said. *Was his pride hurt?*

'Oh Frank, you can call on me whenever you like. You know I will be happy to see you, and I will be home most of the time. I still have a broken arm to mend, you know.'

'I just thought you might be planning to go out with someone else,' he said.

There it was. It was out at last. Frank is jealous of Stan. Carol didn't blame Frank for being jealous. In fact, some women would take that as a compliment. She realised that Frank cared enough to be jealous, and that her relationship with Stan was complicated to say the least, but she did not want to cut Stan off just because Frank had come into her life.

'What do you mean, Frank?' Carol asked.

'Are you going to go out with Stan?' Frank said tersely while placing Carol's bags in the hallway.

'Well, Stan and Billy have asked Jean and me to go to an afternoon matinee at the Regent Theatre. Does that count, Frank?'

'Well …'

'I think the main interest will be how Jean and Billy get on. Jean seems to like Billy, and she needs someone like him in her life right now. Being so close to her child's birth and all. You understand that. Don't you, Frank?'

'Yes. I guess so. I don't suppose I could come along as well?'

'You see, Frank, I want this to be an opportunity for Billy and Jean to hit it off. If you come along there might be tension between you and Stan, which would spoil it for Billy and Jean.'

'Yes. I can see that,' Frank said, turning and walking towards the door. Carol followed him. He stopped at the gate and turned to face Carol. 'I guess either Stan or I would be the odd one out, but tell me Carol, do you love Stan? Would you prefer to be with him? Please be honest with me. Don't drag this out any longer. Just tell me straight where I stand.'

'Golly, you do come straight to the point, don't you.'

'Yes, and I want you to be as straight with me as I am with you.'

'Well, Stan and I have been such good friends for such a long time, but you know that already. Don't you, Frank?'

Frank nodded. 'Yes. And I'm still waiting for an answer,' he said.

'I guess I do, Frank. In a way I do love Stan. He has been very close and dear to me for such a long time, but I do love you too, Frank. I don't expect you to understand what I'm trying to say, but I guess I love both of you. You make my life interesting. I feel alive when I am with you, but I feel safe and secure when I am with Stan. We have so much in common – a shared history. I guess I am very confused about all this, and the accident has made it even more clouded.'

'Ah ha,' Frank said, nodding his head, then dropping it to one side and shaking it. 'You really make it difficult for me, Carol,' he finally said, as he made his way to the Jeep, and got in behind the steering wheel. 'I value the times we have spent together, and I will hold out for you to come back to me. I am not going to give up on you, Carol, but I do not want to share you with anyone else. I can't understand how things have changed between us. We used to be so close.'

'I wish I knew what to say, Frank, so that I don't lose your friendship, but I must insist on keeping Stan's friendship too, and right now that means keeping in touch with both of you.'

'My friendship? So, we are back to being friends, are we? I think it would probably be best if we broke off our engagement and gave each other some time to reflect on what we truly want. What do you think, Carol?'

'Well, if that's what you want, Frank. We could do that, or we could continue seeing each other, and let this work itself out.'

'I don't think it is going to work itself out, Carol, if we don't do something to force a decision. I don't like indecision, so I think it's best if we don't see each other for a while, given how things now stand between us.'

'If that's how you want it, Frank. But please don't think any less of me. You did tell me to be straight with you.'

'Yes, I did, and you have been. You certainly have been that.'

Frank fired up the Jeep's engine and pulled out from

the curb. He did not wave as he left like he usually did. Carol was left standing on the curb with her hand in the air.

*

Although the cast had been removed from Stan's leg, it remained sore, so he used a walking stick to take some of his weight while it improved. The doctor said this was usual for a knee to recover. It was, however, sufficiently healed for Stan to return to work.

One Saturday afternoon, Stan, Billy, Carol and Jean went to a matinee. They took a taxi to the Regent Theatre in Queen Street because of the advanced stage of Jean's pregnancy. Jean had insisted that they all go before the baby was born as she was tired of sitting at home all day every day.

The Regent Theatre in Brisbane was built in 1929 and was designed for both showing films and putting on live productions. It boasted high walls with an arched ceiling in an impressive mixture of Gothic and Empire period styles. The chandelier and elliptical dome in the auditorium gave it a lush finish.

On the afternoon that they went to the matinee, there was a live variety production featuring George

Wallace, Australia's leading comedian, who came on with a straight man. 'You know I'm a great poet,' Wallace said to his companion, who answered, 'No. Really? Recite one of your poems then.'

'Ok. Let's see. Ah, yes. I knew a dame first-class.[3] She was in water up to her ankles,' said George.

'That's not poetry,' his companion protested. 'It doesn't rhyme.'

'Oh, no? Well wait until the tide comes in.'

The audience burst into laughter and were kept laughing as the couple continued their friendly banter. When the dancing girls came on, the men and ladies in the audience cheered at their disciplined routine. A magician also appeared with the usual card and wand tricks. All in all, it was a great success, and Jean and Billy were happy with their afternoon out with Carol and Stan.

After the show they went to the Victory Café for afternoon tea. They ordered scones with their tea and were given jam and cream to go with the scones. They were all enjoying their tea when Frank walked in with some of his buddies.

Carol immediately got to her feet and left the café. Stan followed her, but had trouble keeping up, it being

---

3   In Australia, 'dame' was a term commonly used by working-class people at this time to describe a woman who thought she was better than her peers, or in some cases, who considered 'herself as being of the upper class. Dame was actually a title given to some women of noble birth in England.

awkward with his cane. Frank said nothing as Carol and Stan passed him, but his stare was murderous.

Jean asked Billy to wait at the table and went outside to see what the trouble was. Carol explained to her that she wanted her and Billy to be alone and enjoy the time together, and that she and Stan would go home now.

'It's just that I thought Frank's presence had upset you, Carol. Do you want me to stay with you for a while?' Jean asked.

'No, Jean. Please go back inside with Billy and enjoy your evening out alone.'

Jean returned inside as Frank emerged from the café. 'Please leave Carol alone,' Jean pleaded with Frank, who ignored her and pushed past. 'So, Stan has honoured us with his presence. How's it goin', *mate?*' he said sarcastically.

Carol turned on Frank. 'I thought we had agreed that you would not interfere with Jean and Billy's outing together, Frank.'

'Did I know you would be here? I just happened to be here with a few buddies. You can't blame me for that.'

'What's this all about, Carol?' Stan asked, with anger rising in his tone.

Frank began advancing aggressively towards Stan when Carol stepped in between them.

'Please wait at the corner for me, Stan. I won't be long,' she said. Stan held his ground, and for a minute Carol thought his temper would explode. 'Please, Stan. For my sake. Please go to the corner.'

Frank sneered at Stan, as Stan disengaged and walked away. Carol could see that Stan was very angry and upset, and that it was taking all his self-control to walk away. 'You really have a problem with our whole relationship. Don't you, Frank?'

'Yes, Carol. I really do. How long do you expect me to wait for you to make up your mind?'

'It's only been a few days since our agreement. I think I need more time. If you want to break it off altogether right now, we can.'

'No, Carol. No. I don't want that.'

Frank was cooling down and becoming contrite. 'I can see it was a mistake to come here, but you had better know that I want you, and that I won't wait forever.'

'Yes. I understand that, Frank.'

They separated and Frank went back inside to join his buddies, while Carol joined Stan at the corner for their walk home.

*

Days later, Jean and Billy walked into the lounge room of the Sutton's home where Carol and Stan were sitting and chatting. 'Oh Jean, there's a letter for you from that American captain.' Carol pointed to the letter resting on the occasional table in front of her.

Jean picked up the letter and reached for a chair to pull up to the occasional table to rest her legs on. Billy could see what Jean was trying to do, so he also reached for the chair. 'Here, let me do that for you, Jean,' he said, and pulled the chair up to the table.

Jean sat down, put her legs up and read the letter. She looked up at Carol. 'Ben said that the government wants a blood test done on the baby,' she said. 'I guess I'll have to go to the hospital and arrange it tomorrow. They can take blood from the baby when it's in my belly, can't they?'

'I'm not sure,' Carol replied. 'But can't you wait until after you have the baby. It's due anytime now.'

'I suppose. But Ben did say that it takes a long time to process my claim. I don't want to keep him waiting.'

'Can't you write to Ben and tell him you want to wait until the baby is born?'

'I guess that's best. I don't want to do anything that might harm the baby while it's in my belly. Ok then. That's what I'll do.'

CHAPTER 11

Billy saw a lot of Jean over the coming weeks, during which time they became very close friends. Carol was happy to see Jean beginning to enjoy herself again. One late summer evening, when Carol, Jean and Billy were sitting on their porch, Jean felt her water break and her contractions start.

'I need to get to the hospital, Carol. It's time.'

Things became hectic for a while, as Carol rushed to a neighbour's place and called for an ambulance, and Jean gathered her things together. They had packed Jean's bags in anticipation of this event, but now they went over everything while waiting for the ambulance. In this way, Carol tried to occupy Jean's mind to keep her from contemplating the ordeal ahead. However, Carol soon ran out of things to say. Billy was standing next to Jean, not knowing what to do, but holding her hand for comfort. There was an awkward silence as Carol searched her mind for something to say.

'Do you think the ambulance will make it, Carol?' Jean asked.

'It always has before,' Carol replied.

'But there wasn't a war before.'

Billy tried to relax Jean by adding, 'True. But things are a bit easier now, Jean. The Japs are further away, and there are not as many soldiers here now.'

'Yes. That's right,' Carol affirmed. There was another awkward silence. 'Perhaps I should go and get Mrs Taylor,' Carol offered.

'Yes. Do, please,' pleaded Jean, a nervous strain in her voice.

Carol made a quick dash down the street to Stan's house, and within minutes, Stan and Esmay had arrived. Esmay took charge right away. 'How far apart are the contractions, dear,' she asked Jean.

'We haven't timed them, but they are getting closer now,' Carol replied.

'I see. Billy, get Jean a clock so she can time how far apart the pains are. Carol, you go and boil some water – lots of it – and get a raincoat and clean sheet for me. Stan, help me get Jean into the bedroom.'

Esmay stripped the bed down, then laid the raincoat on the mattress and put a clean sheet over the raincoat and mattress. She tucked the sheet in tight. After Billy had returned with the clock, she asked the boys to help put Jean onto the bed. When Jean was settled, Esmay put a pillow behind the small of Jean's back and turned to the boys. 'Right … you boys, out of here and don't come back until you are called for.'

'Anything else?' Carol asked as she returned from the kitchen.

'I'll need two pegs and a pair of strong scissors, which need to be boiled for twenty minutes.'

'Right,' said Carol as she headed for the kitchen again.

Stan left Billy in the lounge and went to see Carol in the kitchen. He found her putting the pegs and scissors into a large pot of boiling water. 'Mum seems to know what she is doing,' he said.

'Yes. And we are very grateful for her help, but I still hope the ambulance will arrive before it's too late.'

Billy couldn't stay on his own, so he went back into the bedroom and held Jean's hand. He felt useless, but his presence seemed to comfort Jean, so Esmay said nothing. The contractions were seven minutes apart by the time the ambulance arrived and transported Jean to the hospital.

They all took a taxi to the maternity ward and waited for word from the delivery room. Nothing much was said between them as they all went into their own private thoughts. As for Carol, she began to reflect on whose baby she would want to carry – Stan's or Frank's.

Carol wondered who would make the better father for her child. They were both strong-willed men and capable of caring for their child, but she wondered what Frank would be like after the war, especially if they moved to America. That part she didn't like. Also, Stan had been a life-long friend, and she had loved him for a long time. On the other hand, Stan kept saying how he had changed because of the war, but she had seen Billy with Jean, and they were fine. Eventually, she got tired of her mind going round in circles and began to think of what Jean was going through. 'Do you think Jean will be ok, Mrs Taylor?' Carol asked.

'Oh yes, dear. Don't worry. We will hear from the doctor any time now.'

After the birth, they all went into the maternity ward to see Jean, who looked exhausted, but nevertheless smiled with satisfaction. Billy smiled back as he took Jean's hand, and his eyes reflected his joy. 'My word, Jean,' he said, 'you have your own child now.'

'Yes, Billy. It's a girl. Do you like girls?'

'Oh sure. Doesn't matter to me. Boys or girls. They're all new life, and that's what counts.'

He bent over and kissed Jean on the forehead. Carol could see the happiness between Jean and Billy, and knew right away that she wanted them to be together as they raised her niece.

The next day, Jean's doctor came to see her during his rounds. He took the clipboard from the end of her bed and examined the notes recorded there. Then, he looked up and smiled at Jean. 'Well, young lady, you appear to be doing fine. How do you feel?'

'I'm feeling pretty good thank you, Doctor.'

'Good. Well, your blood pressure and pulse rate are fine. You have some bleeding but that should stop with a little rest. Do you feel any pain?'

'Yes, Doctor. I have some pain in my … you know … down there.'

The doctor gave a little chuckle. 'Some women have a little pain, but not to worry. It's just your uterus contracting to its pre-birth size.'

'Oh. I see.'

'Yes. We'll keep you in here for a few days to keep an eye on you. You probably could use the rest. I hear you're a waitress, is that right?'

'Yes. That's right.'

'You'll have to take a break from that for a couple of weeks at least. Try and get plenty of rest and keep off your feet as much as possible. If your feet start to swell up, you'll have to elevate them. Lay down on the bed and put something under them to raise them above your heart. The swelling will just be fluid accumulating in your legs, so you need to help it drain away, but you might not have to worry about that. We'll just have to wait and see.'

Jean told him about her claim with the US government for Johnny's insurance. The doctor looked on with sympathy as Jean told him that Johnny had died, and how she was now left with his child.

'So, you see, the US government wants a blood test done on my child to check that she is Johnny's child. Could I have that done before I leave the hospital, please?'

'Certainly. I'll do it myself. I'll make three copies so you can send two to your lawyer and keep one for yourself. Do you have a name for your child yet? I'll need a name for the blood test.'

'Yes. It's Lynda. I've always loved that name.'

They both smiled at each other before the doctor took his leave. 'Don't worry about any of this. I'll make sure you get what you want before we let you go,' he said as he left.

*

Some weeks after Jean had returned home with Lynda, Carol was sitting outside on the front verandah. She was alone because Jean was out walking with Lynda. With her arm still in a cast, Carol had had time to reflect on all that had happened to her over the past year. She was grateful that she now had a baby niece, and like all aunts, she was sure she would spoil Lynda. Things would be hard for a while with an extra mouth to feed. Then there were all the costs that would mount up as Lynda grew. Jean had already returned to work, but until she could return to work as well there was a heavy strain on their family budget. It would be better for Lynda if Billy and Jean were to marry. *A child needs a mother and father to look up to as he or she grows.* Carol reflected on how much she had missed her own mother, and how she had tried so hard to be a substitute mother for Jean. She felt Stan must have had a similar time growing up without a father.

Carol sighed and leaned back deep into the chair. Jean seemed to like Billy, and he seemed to return her affection. She was so happy for her sister, and grateful, once again, for Stan, who had sided with her in bringing Jean and Billy together. Jean had been talking to her about the possibility of getting married to Billy, and Carol had told her to be patient, but also to have a conversation with Billy about marriage generally. Carol suggested just simply bring up the topic in a general way and let it hang there for Billy to take it further if he wanted. It warmed Carol's heart to know that the two of them might one day get married and start a family together.

The problem of Stan and Frank, however, remained on her mind. She began to believe that she had somehow been unfair to Frank. After all, she still hadn't broken her engagement to him. They had agreed to stay apart for a short time, and Frank was perfectly within his rights to resent Stan.

The more she thought about it, the more she felt she needed to call Frank and try to explain her position better. To somehow get Frank to see things from her perspective, so she left the house and walked down to the nearest public telephone at the end of their street.

Frank had given her a telephone number that he said would reach him in case of emergency. She dialled it, and a duty sergeant came on the other end.

'Signals, Sergeant Williams speaking.'

'Hello Sergeant. I'm Carol Sutton and Sergeant Frank Brooks gave me this number to contact him. Is he available please?'

'You have the right number, Miss Sutton, but unfortunately Sergeant Brooks is not here right now. Can I take a message, or get him to call you back?'

'No. Thank you. I'll call again later. Can you tell me

when you expect him to be in?'

'That's a little hard to say. Why don't you call back tomorrow at this time. I'm pretty sure he will be in then.'

'Thank you, Sergeant. Goodbye.'

The duty sergeant hung up the phone and turned to Frank. 'Hey, Frank. That Sutton chick just called. I told her to call back tomorrow, like you wanted me to.'

'Thanks, Greg. Let her squirm a little. It always makes them come to their senses.' Frank grinned and clapped his hands in delight.

Carol walked back up the hill and returned to the verandah. Her arm itched from the heat of the walk. She grabbed a ruler that she kept handy and poked it down the inside of the half-cast on her forearm. Relief came instantly.

The next day, Carol called again and was put through to Frank.

'Hello, Carol. What can I do for you?' he asked.

'Oh. Nothing, Frank. I'm just calling to find out how you are doing.'

'I'm fine, Carol.' Frank stopped there, waiting for Carol to say something.

'I just wanted to know that you are not upset with me, Frank. You seemed upset the last time we met, and I know this must be hard on you.'

'Not especially, Carol. I'm still waiting for you to make up your mind about us.'

'Yes, Frank. I was hoping we could still be friends.'

'So, you don't want to be engaged to me anymore?'

'Well, it's not the same as before is it, Frank? I was just hoping that you could understand my position a bit better now. Now that we have had time apart.'

'Sure. Does that mean you want to end our relationship?'

'Oh. No, Frank. Nothing like that. I still like you a lot. I still want us to be friends.'

'But we are not just friends, are we, Carol? We are a lot more than that. You don't seem to understand that you promised yourself to me. I can't let you go. You belong to me now. I'm not going to give you up without a fight.'

'Just a minute, Frank. I don't belong to anyone. I can make up my own mind about what I want.'

'Sure. Anything else, Carol?'

'No. That's all I called about, Frank.'

'Well, I'm pretty busy here, so if there's nothing else, I'll say goodbye.'

'Yes, Frank. Good …'

Frank hung up and Carol heard a loud click that cut her off. It sounded so definite and somehow menacing.

She had hoped for a better result from her phone call and was not happy with Frank's response. She knew that Frank was still angry with her for what had happened between them, but there was nothing she could do about that now. She had to leave Frank alone, and hope that he overcame his disappointment in her.

Well, she told herself, *I have a couple of more weeks in this cast, so I'd better find something to do with myself, and stop thinking about the past.*

*

Carol spent the next few weeks looking after her niece, Lynda. She took her out for walks in a stroller that a kind neighbour had loaned them, because, as the neighbour put it, she was in between babies. They went to the parks around Brisbane where Carol enjoyed the sunshine as much as Lynda. Carol also went to the local library to take some books out on loan. Jean, who had wanted to return to work, even though she was still nursing her baby, would express her milk and leave it in bottles for Carol to make up Lynda's daily feeding. Between the two of them, they made Lynda's life as pleasant as it could be.

Carol would also wait on the verandah for Stan to

return from work. He would stop by and the two of them would sit and chat about the day's events. This was Carol's favourite time of the day. Sometimes she would fantasise that Lynda was their daughter, and Stan was coming home to the two of them.

Frank, on the other hand, was furious with Carol. *The nerve of that woman to call me and try to pity me. So condescending, so patronising.*

On the day she had called, he had banged the receiver down so hard that Sergeant Williams had looked up from what he was doing. 'What's up, Frank?' he had asked.

'Nothing,' Frank had replied, 'just some silly talk that was wasting my time.'

Frank vowed to himself that he would show Carol not to play games with him. The next time she called he would be ready. He wouldn't let her get away with that again. *Nobody treats Frank Brooks like that. How dare she leave me for another man? I'll show her, that's for sure. Anyway, who does she think she is? She's just a waitress after all. It's not as though she's somebody important. There're plenty more like her around. Fancy someone like her making a fool of Frank Brooks! So, if she thinks she can leave me for another man, after promising herself to me, maybe I'll have something to say about that.*

However, Carol never did call him again, so Frank's anger festered. He could not confront her again, and the anger kept growing. Somehow, he told himself, he would put Carol in her place, but the real problem for Frank was that he still loved her, and his jealousy of Stan also grew into a monster he could not control.

*

After Carol's arm came out of its cast and she had returned to work, life settled back into a regular rhythm. Billy acquired a job with Stan in the Lands Office and the two of them walked to work with Carol; Jean, being on another shift at work meant she could not join them. However, Carol insisted that Stan not walk all the way with her to the café because of his leg. Although he no longer wrapped his knee in crepe bandages, he was still walking with a cane.

Carol was content to see Stan every day. She wanted so much to draw a commitment of love from him; they had, in fact, skirted this topic on many occasions, but nothing concrete had come of it. Carol sensed that Stan loved her and wanted her, but he remained uncommitted while Frank lingered in the background. Carol knew she would have to end it with Frank if she wanted Stan to commit to her, and this made her more determined than ever before to confront Frank and end their relationship.

*

One day, Stan and Billy were sitting on the verandah of Stan's home having a beer, when Billy suddenly turned the conversation to his relationship with Jean.

'You know, Stan? I really love Jean, and I'm crazy about Lynda. She's so … new, so perfect. It's so good to see new life after all the death we witnessed. They have brought sunshine back into my life.'

He said it straight out and caught Stan by surprise, who took a few moments to gather his thoughts before replying. 'Well … I guess I sort of knew that, Billy. You seem to enjoy yourself when you're around them.'

'Yes. You know, mate, it has made such a difference to me. I want to be with them for the rest of my life. Do you think I should ask Jean to marry me?'

Stan took an even longer time to respond this time. 'I don't know, mate. That's a big step.' Stan put his hand up to his chin and turned to face Billy. 'You know I don't like to give advice on matters of the heart. You never know how things will work out. I don't want to lose your friendship if something goes wrong, mate. I hope you understand.'

'Oh, sure. I understand, Stan. But can you just tell me your thoughts. I won't take it as advice, and I won't hold it against you later if things don't work out.'

'Well … Just let me say this. Like me, you have been left with a lot of problems since Kokoda. Have you explained it all thoroughly to Jean?'

'Oh, yes. Don't worry about that. I'm much better now. Coming up here to be with you and your mum, and Jean and Carol, has made a big difference in my life, and I'm even on lighter doses of my medication now. Jean and I have talked about it, and she even went with me to one of my sessions with my psychiatrist. He told her all about the problems I am having from my war experience. He told her that I would probably fall into periods of depression from time to time, and that she would need to understand what I was going through. He told her that she could always call him for advice at any time she needed it. That seemed to comfort her a lot.'

Billy stopped and took a deep breath. 'Jean understands, mate. She really does. I guess she feels she owes me something for the way I have taken to her daughter. My word, Stan, I really do love them so much, and they have made such a big difference in my life.'

Billy held his hands together between his knees and looked straight ahead out onto the road. It seemed like he was searching for something more to say, so Stan put his hand on his shoulder and said, 'You know, Billy? You are a very lucky man. You might have a chance to really make a go of things. I wish you all the best, mate.'

'Thanks Stan. And I do know how lucky I am. I really do.'

*

Billy continued calling on Jean and asking her out. The two of them went to the movies and on picnics together with Lynda. Sometimes Billy would hold Lynda in his arms, and she would snuggle in close to his chest. Billy felt so moved by this that he would smile and rock her gently. Jean felt that Billy loved her child, and she began to see a future for the three of them, and now that she had returned to work, she was determined to confess her love for him. Even though she didn't want to rush into another relationship like she had done with Johnny, she knew that Lynda needed a father. At times, she felt that Billy was going to say something to her about marriage, but then he always looked away and rubbed his hand across his forehead. She wondered if he was just shy or afraid of rejection.

Now that Carol had returned to work, it was perfect for Jean, because they had taken different shifts and that left one of them at home to look after Lynda. She had asked Carol if that arrangement would suit her and Carol had replied, 'Of course, we are family, and look after one another.'

When Jean started back at work, she had mixed feeling about it. On the one hand, she knew that the family budget needed the extra income she provided, and she did enjoy the company she had with the other girls at work. On the other hand, the work was tiring and repetitive, and it kept her away from Lynda. She always missed Lynda when she was away from her. She would return home from work tired, but always went straight to Lynda's crib, and stood looking down at her until the joy she felt in being with her daughter drove the tiredness from her body.

One night, Billy and Jean went to a dance at Cloudland while Carol and Stan stayed home with Lynda. Jean was so excited about going to a dance after such a long time and she skipped across the floor to their seats. Billy laughed at her light-heartedness and joined in. They fell into each other's arms with laughter.

They danced until they became too tired to dance anymore, so Billy got them a drink and they went outside to the cool of the evening. 'My word, Jean, you are a great dancer,' Billy said.

'You're not so bad yourself, Billy.'

'Well, I try to keep up with you.' They drifted into a short silence, sipping their drinks and catching their breath. 'Do you want to know something, Jean?'

'What, Billy?'

'I love you, Jean. I love you and I want to marry you and take care of you and Lynda.'

'Gosh, Billy. Just like that.'

Jean had been taken by surprise. Billy had finally confessed his true feelings to her. A sense of joy filled her heart, and a broad smile lit up her face. The time had arrived when she could confess her feelings for him too. She wanted so much to rush in and accept his proposal, but she wanted to be sure about the depth of Billy's commitment.

'Oh, Billy. I do love you too. And I know how good you and Lynda are together. But do you really want to take on the responsibility for another man's child?'

'Why do you ask that? Can't you see how much I love both of you? I know I'm not just marrying you, Jean. I know you come with Lynda. I fully accept the responsibility that comes with marrying you, and I would be proud to call Lynda my daughter. I wish you could see that and believe in me.'

'Gosh, Billy, I do believe you. I just wanted to be sure that you know what you're getting into. That's all. You are kind and considerate and fun to be with. I do love you, Billy, and I do want to marry you.'

They stood facing each other, holding hands and smiling broadly at each other.

'Is that all?' Jean asked.

'What do you mean? Did I miss something?'

'Aren't you going to get down on your knee? A girl likes to remember that sort of thing you know.'

'How silly of me, Jean,' Billy said, hitting his forehead with the butt of his hand. 'I forgot. My mind got so mixed up just now.' Billy reached into his pocket, took out an engagement ring, and got down on one knee.

'Jean Sutton, will you marry me?' he said confidently.

'Oh, yes, Billy. I will. With pleasure.'

*

Coming home to Lynda only to eat and sleep, and having to leave her in the morning for the whole day, often left Jean feeling that she was not doing right by her daughter or herself. That was why she was looking forward to her marriage to Billy and more time with Lynda.

Jean and Billy continued enjoying each other's company. When Jean was on a day shift, Billy would walk her to work each morning and then go back to his own work in the Lands Office. When Jean finished her shift, and Billy was not working, he would go to the Victory Café and walk her home. Jean liked Billy's attention to her needs, and she realised he was always there for her and Lynda. *I'm so lucky,* she told herself. She was, nevertheless, going through a terrible time waiting for the three weeks to pass before the wedding. She kept worrying that something would go wrong and leave her alone again without Billy, just as it had done with Johnny.

Finally, the day arrived. They had a small ceremony with just a few family members and friends. Stan was Billy's best man, and both of them stood nervously awaiting the arrival of the bride. When Jean appeared, she was simply radiant in her gown and veil. As Jean's father walked her down the aisle, Stan's mother started to cry, and wiped her nose with a handkerchief. Carol too had to wipe a tear from her eye.

After their marriage, and short honeymoon, Billy and Jean arrived back home to a welcoming from Jean's father and Carol. Jean went straight to Lynda and picked her up. A big smile lit up Lynda's face, and Jean's eyes welled up with joy. It was decided that Billy would move in with Jean and Lynda into the large bedroom, and Alan would take one of the smaller rooms. It was a bit cramped but a good arrangement for everyone because they all got on so well. Alan was not home very much because he worked so late, and he often spent his time out with his mates at the pub, drinking and listening to the horse races. He didn't gamble much but occasionally had a bet. If he had a win, he always brought home fish and chips for everyone, which made the whole house happy. He was glad that Jean had married, which had provided a father for Lynda. There were no bad tempers in the house, and everyone was cheerful, so the arrangement worked well for all of them.

*

One day, when Billy, Jean and Lynda were at the Botanic Gardens on a picnic, Jean turned to Billy. 'Do you want me to keep working, Billy?'

'Well, that's up to you, Jean. Do you want to?'

'Not really. I would rather spend more time with Lynda.'

'Well, don't then. You can give up work whenever you like.'

'Um … It's just that I don't want to have to keep paying rent like Dad has done his whole life. I know how much he had to sacrifice for Carol and me now that we are keeping a family budget of our own. I owe Dad so much, and I didn't make it easy for him growing up.'

Jean put her hands on the side of her head and stroked her forehead with her fingers. Billy moved over and wrapped his arms around her. 'I know your dad loves you, and I'm sure he was happy to make the sacrifice he did. As for your growing up, don't feel guilty. It will only make you unhappy, and I know your father would not want that for you. Don't you think he would rather see you happy?'

'Yes. You are right,' Jean said, dropping her hands, straightening her back, and pulling back her shoulders. 'Anyway, I thought that if I kept working, we could save enough to buy a block of land and put a deposit on a home. Then we would have a place of our own. What do you think?'

'That sounds like a good idea.' Billy laughed.

'Why are you laughing?'

'Because I have some money that I have put away for us. My pay and demob cheque from the army that

I left in the bank is still there, and I have added to that with some savings since I started work. I have enough to buy a block of land right now. We could go look at some land sales next weekend if you like.'

'You ...' Jean pushed Billy to the ground and straddled his stomach. She started to tickle him, and the two of them laughed at each other.

'You ... beautiful thing ... you ...' She ran out of words, then bent her head down and kissed him on the lips. 'Oops ... should we do that in public?' she asked cheekily.

Lynda pumped her arms up and down before crawling over to her parents and resting her head on Billy's chest.

CHAPTER 12

Frank's relationship with Carol had now become an obsession with him. Ever since he had suggested that they give each other time to work it out, things had gone from bad to worse, and now he hadn't heard from her in weeks. He had expected her to come back to him with her arms open, but that hadn't happened. After all that they had promised each other, he couldn't accept that she might want someone else over him.

He had become jealous of Stan, and this had led to a dangerous obsession over Carol. Frank couldn't get her out of his mind, but he did not want to confront her for fear of losing her, so he had just stayed away, hoping that she would come back to him. He knew he would never let her go and loathed what she was putting him through. Somehow, some way, he was convinced that this stand-off would have to stop, and Carol would marry him. Frank could not contemplate any other resolution to their relationship.

When Carol's arm had come out of its cast, and she had returned to work, Frank began to stalk her. He watched her walk to and from work with Stan. They were always talking and laughing and enjoying each other's company. He hated what he saw and hated himself for being reduced to spying on Carol, but he felt she had left him with no other option.

Finally, he came to believe he would lose her if he didn't do something, so he waited one night for Carol to come off the evening shift, when she would be alone. He pulled her aside outside the Victory Café.

'Oh! It's you, Frank,' Carol exclaimed as he took her arm and squeezed it hard. 'Please let go of my arm. You are hurting me.'

'I didn't mean to hurt you, but I had to see you.'

'Yes, Frank. I've been wanting to see you too.'

'Yes. Are you ready to come back to me now? There is so much I want to do with you, Carol. We could take a few days off and go to Scarborough if you like or take a drive into the country and stay in a quiet country town. Anything you want is good by me.'

'Frank, I don't know how to say this.'

Frank stamped his foot. 'Then don't say it, Carol,' he yelled. 'Just tell me everything is the same as it was, and that you want to go away with me,' he pleaded.

'Frank. I …'

'Don't do it, Carol. Don't say it. You belong to me.

You are mine forever. I told you that I love you and want to marry you, and nothing you do or say will ever change me. I am that sort of guy. I don't change, Carol, and I never will.'

'Oh dear.'

'So, where do you want to go? Scarborough or the country?'

'Frank. I don't want to go anywhere with you …'

'No! No! No! You don't get to say that, Carol.'

Frank stamped his foot again and put his hands up to his face, wiping them across to the side of his head. He kept his eyes closed and held his head in his hands. 'Why are you doing this, Carol? What did I do to deserve this? To change your mind … your heart? You did love me once, didn't you?' Frank put his hands on Carol's shoulders.

'I told you, Frank. I thought that Stan was dead when …'

'Stan. Stan. Stan,' interrupted Frank as he began to shake Carol's shoulders. 'Oh yes. Wonder boy Stan. Stan the great. Where does that leave me? I can't let you do this to me, Carol.'

Another American soldier, who had noticed their dispute, stepped up to them. 'Are you ok, ma'am?' he asked.

'Yes. Thank you. It's just that we are sharing some bad news.'

'Ok, ma'am. If you need me, I'll be just over here.'

'Shove off, Mack. Before you get hurt,' hissed Frank.

The American soldier turned towards Frank.

'Please. We are ok. Really. Please let us work it out,' Carol pleaded as she stood between them. The American soldier moved to the brick wall behind them, leaning his back on it and raising one leg behind to rest his foot against it.

'I am sorry, Frank. So sorry.' Carol put her hand in her pocket and withdrew Frank's engagement ring. She opened her hand and offered it to him. 'I'm so sorry, Frank. Please forgive me.'

Frank slapped her hard in the face, and the ring flew out of her hand.

'Oh!' Carol exclaimed, with surprise.

'I'm sorry, Carol. Please don't ...' Frank began to explain.

That was all that Frank could say before the other American soldier slammed his fist into Frank's face. Frank staggered backward but kept his footing. He wiped his mouth with the back of his hand.

'Please don't do that,' Carol pleaded. 'You don't know what is going on between us.'

'Nobody hits a woman when I'm around, ma'am,' the American soldier said.

Frank drove his shoulder into the soldier's stomach and pinned him against the brick wall. Then, he straightened and began to pummel the soldier. They both went at each other with body blows and head punches.

Carol stepped up again. 'Stop this!' she screamed. 'Please stop this immediately. Please. Both of you … stop this!' She tried to pull them apart – they both stopped, and Frank turned to face Carol as she pleaded, 'Why are you doing this, Frank? Can't you just accept that it's over?'

'I don't want to end our relationship like this, Carol. Please say you will see me again,' Frank implored.

The other American soldier stood his ground, waiting to see what happened next.

'No, Frank. What we had is over now. I am sorry it took me so long to reach this point, but I am now convinced that we have no future together. I guess you're not yourself right now, and I can understand that, but that does not give you the right to hit me and try to beat up this poor young man, who was just concerned about my safety.'

'Yes. Yes. You are right, Carol,' Frank said. 'I'm

sorry. I'll never do that again, but you must stay with me.' Frank retrieved the engagement ring and tried to put it back on Carol's finger, but Carol kept her hand clenched.

'Hey, Buddy. Can't you see she doesn't want you anymore? Why not leave her alone? Let her go, and find someone else,' said Frank's adversary, with a hint of sympathy for him. Frank turned to face him, and they both took up fighting positions.

'Please don't fight over me anymore. You are both making me feel uncomfortable.'

'Then come back to me, Carol. Come back and make it right for both of us.'

'No, Frank. It's over. Please accept that.'

'No, Carol. You don't get to walk away that easily. I don't accept this. It's Stan, isn't it? He has filled your head with lies, and has you infatuated with him.'

'It's you, Frank, who is obsessed. Not Stan. Please accept what I say and stay away from me.'

'Oh, you'll see me again, Carol. You can count on that.' With that said, he turned and hurried away. The other American soldier stood looking at Carol.

'I'm sorry about this, ma'am. I hope you don't hold this against all Americans. Because of one bad apple, I mean.' He paused for a moment, then went on. 'I don't think you have seen the last of him though, and I wish there was more I could do for you, but I'll be shipping out soon. Perhaps you should go to the police. Maybe they can help you.'

'I don't think so, but thanks for your concern. You have been a perfect gentleman, and I don't hold anything against Americans. What has happened between Frank and me is both our fault. It has nothing to do with you or your country.'

'Yes, ma'am,' he said. They stood together in silence. 'My name is James Brown,' he eventually said.

'I'm Carol Sutton,' Carol said, extending her hand in friendship. They smiled and shook hands.

'I'm still worried about you, ma'am. Can I walk you home? Just to be safe, I mean.'

Carol thought about his offer. She was still a little shaken by what had happened and could do with someone's company on the walk home. Since Stan and Billy had gone out for the night, she was all alone now. 'I live about thirty minutes from here, and it is a fairly steep, uphill climb. It's up there on Spring Hill. Are you sure you want to walk with me?'

'Oh sure. That sort of walk doesn't bother me, and I'd feel a lot better if you were to let me walk you home. It's just that I'm a little worried for your safety, you see.'

'Yes, then. Thank you. I am grateful for your offer.'

'Yes, ma'am.'

They walked in silence for a time, then Carol opened up a conversation. 'Do you like it here in Australia?' she asked.

'Oh, sure. Australia reminds me a lot of home back in Tennessee.'

'Oh, whereabouts in Tennessee are you from?'

'Nashville, ma'am. Have you heard about Nashville?'

'Yes. That's where all the country music singers come from, isn't it?'

He laughed at this. 'Well, a lot of them sing there. That's for sure. We have the Grand Ole Opry, you see. That's a concert hall where the country singers perform. They all make a big fuss about it.'

'Oh yes. I've heard about that. Have you been there?'

'Sure. I think all Nashville folks, if not all Tennesseans, have been there.' He smiled down at Carol.

Carol thought, *What a really nice young man this man from Tennessee is.*

'Bris-bane reminds me a lot of Nashville. They're both just big country towns full of friendly people. Don't you think?'

Carol smiled about the way that he had pronounced Brisbane. Most Americans seemed to pronounce it that way. 'Well, I've never been to Nashville, so I'll have to take your word for it, but I'm happy that you see us as friendly.'

'Oh sure. I've never met an Aussie I didn't like. Aussies are a lot like us really.'

They walked on and continued chatting about their hometowns until they reached Carol's home. 'Well, this is where I live. Thank you so much for walking me home tonight. I have really enjoyed it.'

'Yes, ma'am. I'm happy to have been of service to you. I do hope you will think kindly of us Americans, and I'm sorry about what happened to you tonight.'

'You have been a perfect gentleman, and a fine example for your country. Thank you once again.' Carol offered her hand, and the young American took it.

'Well, goodnight, ma'am. I hope it all works out for you.' With that, he turned and walked away.

Carol stood looking down at the footpath as mixed emotions flowed over her. She had been so impressed by the young man from Nashville, but when she thought about Frank, a cold shiver ran down her spine. She decided not to tell Stan anything about the incident with Frank, as it would only enflame an already precarious situation, and would probably lead to a confrontation, which was precisely what she was trying to avoid. No.

It was better to just act like nothing had happened and hope that Frank would finally give up and move on.

*

On the walk to work one morning, Stan surprised Carol, when he asked if he could walk her all the way to work. He said he had something he wanted to ask her. Carol agreed and Billy peeled off and headed for the Lands Office. When they were alone Stan stopped and opened up about their relationship. 'Do you think we could maybe make a go of it, Carol?'

'What do you mean, Stan?'

'Well, I've been watching Billy and Jean, and they seem so happy. Do you think we could maybe go for it like them?'

'Oh, Stan. I do love you and I've been waiting to hear that from you.' A big smile crossed Carol's face. *At last, he has said it,* she thought. 'Yes. Yes, Stan. I want to make a go of it too.'

'I thought that the war had changed me too much for happiness and caring for anyone, but with you it's different. I love you too, Carol. I love you and want to be with you for the rest of my life. You know, Billy went through everything I did, and he's game enough to make a go of it, so why can't I?'

'Yes, Stan. That's right.'

'You know, Carol, I'm so happy right now.' Stan stepped forward and embraced Carol, raising her feet off the ground.

'Oh, Stan. We are in public. Wait until we are alone.'

Stan laughed with delight. 'Oh yeah. Sorry, Carol.' He put her down and stepped back. 'What about Frank, Carol? What are we going to do about him?'

'Haven't you noticed that I haven't been wearing his ring for some time now, Stan? It's over between Frank and me. Has been for a while.'

Stan was so pleased; his face broke out in a broad smile. 'I'm so happy to hear that, Carol. I was hoping the way would be clear for us, and now it is.'

They walked on. As they turned the corner into Queen Street, Frank, who had witnessed everything that had passed between Stan and Carol, stepped out of the shadows carrying his .45 service pistol and followed them into the Victory Café.

I'll kill her in the same place where she accepted my proposal of marriage. That will be justice for me. That's the way she will pay for what she has done, Frank argued in his mind.

An American serviceman, who was sitting at a

table allowing him a clear view of the doorway, saw Frank enter the café carrying a pistol. Frank walked in and stopped next to the table where the American serviceman was sitting. Then, Frank raised his .45 and pointed it at Carol's back.

He was about to fire when the American soldier, seeing what was happening, moved with lightning speed. He reached out for Frank's arm, and pulled it down. Frank fired, and the bullet hit Carol in the buttocks. She screamed, falling forward, clutching at her wound.

Frank turned on the soldier, who had grabbed at his arm, and the two of them began to struggle over Frank's weapon. Stan knelt down to check on Carol as more American soldiers subdued Frank and took the .45 from him.

'Let me go!' Frank screamed at those who were holding him down. 'I still have to kill that bitch. She's the one who forced me into this. I didn't want to kill her, but she brought it on herself.'

One of the Americans who was holding Frank down said, 'No, Buddy. You did this, and you will have to face up to it.'

Stan turned and approached the Americans. 'Let the mongrel go,' he said between clenched teeth. 'Let him go so I can have a piece of him.'

Two Australians, who sat at a table next to Stan, looked at each other and nodded. They got up and stood on either side of Stan. Then they grabbed Stan's arms and restrained him. Stan fought against their restraint, but they held him fast.

'Look, mate,' one of them said. 'He's not worth it. You'll only get yourself into trouble if you get into a fight. Let the Yanks have him. They'll punish him more than you ever will.'

'Stan!' Carol called out. 'Come to me. I need you.'

Stan turned his head to look at Carol, and calmed down. 'Yeah. OK. I'm good now. Let me go. I want to get back to my girl.'

The Australians released him and Stan went back to Carol, who was still lying on the floor of the café. She was pressing on her wound in an attempt to stop the bleeding. She looked up at Stan; hurt and sorrow filled her face. 'I'm sorry about this, Stan. I had no idea that Frank would take it this far. That he would do something like this,' Carol said.

Her face was wrinkled in pain as she reached out for Stan with her free hand. He took it and placed his other hand on top of Carol's hand pressing on her wound. 'It's ok, Carol. Nothing is going to spoil this day for me now that we are together. The important thing is to get you some medical help.' Stan looked up at Beryl. 'Has someone called for an ambulance?' he asked.

'Yes, Stan. I told them it was an emergency, and they said they would come right away.'

The American military police arrived first, and when Frank tried to break away from them to get to Carol, they beat Frank mercilessly with their batons and threw him to the ground where they handcuffed his hands behind his back, dragged him to his feet, and took him away. This time, Stan looked on at the MPs' rough handling with a degree of satisfaction.

Shortly after Frank had been taken away, an ambulance came and took Carol to the hospital.

*

The next morning, when Jean arrived at work, Beryl called her over to speak with her. 'I suppose Carol will be off for quite a while.'

'Yes. She is still in hospital, and she'll have to rest up when she returns home.'

'Well, you probably have noticed that things have gotten a lot quieter here since most of the soldiers have left.'

'Yes, Mrs Cooper.'

'I'm going to have to stop the night shift. We don't get enough customers at that time anymore, so I'll have to reduce my staff. I hope Carol will understand, but I have to let her go.'

'Gosh, Mrs Cooper. We need the money that she brings in. Can you reconsider?'

'I'm afraid not, Jean. I have to run a business you know, and there are others who also need the work. It would not be fair on them for me to keep both of you.'

'I see. Well, can she take my place when she is ready to come back?'

'That would be fine by me. You two have been through so much and have been good employees, so I'll definitely keep one of you on here permanently.'

'Thank you, Mrs Cooper, we appreciate that.'

Jean walked towards the kitchen to put on her apron and start work. Beryl Cooper reflected on all that had happened to Carol and Jean. *Poor dears*, she thought, *the war put them through so much.* She remembered how naïve and innocent Jean had been when she first started with her. Beryl thought how Jean was now so mature and considerate. *The war has made everyone grow up fast, and stolen the innocence of so many young ones.* Beryl sighed and began greeting customers entering the café.

EPILOGUE

everal years later, Stan stood on an escarpment that was the Toowoomba Lookout on the edge of the Great Dividing Range. He and Carol had come to Toowoomba for the Carnival of Flowers festival. The rich, vibrant colours of the flowers had moved Stan. He was amazed at the effect the flowers had when cultivated into a garden. They made a splendid sight, which had left him with a calm feeling.

Now he stood looking out on the open expanse that was the Lockyer Valley – the garden basket of Brisbane. He noticed the hills that dotted the landscape and the farming patches along the fertile river valley. Much of the water came from an artesian source, and the farmers used a rotation system of farming, so the farming patches were different shades of green, brown and red. The sky above was a deep, dark-blue, and the tree-lined horizon a lighter pastel blue. Small puffs of cloud moved lazily across the sky, casting shadows on the land below. The whole effect was a humbling one for Stan. He stood in awe of the open vista.

He thought how peaceful it all looked from up here, but knew that down below people were struggling with everyday life, like he and Carol were, now they had married. Billy and Jean had bought a place of their own, so to save on rent Stan and Carol had both moved in with Stan's mother. Since Carol's father was now alone, he too had moved in with them. Stan smiled to himself as he thought about how childlike Carol's father and his mother were, now that they lived together in the same house. They seemed to enjoy each other's company, and Stan even believed that another marriage might be on the horizon.

Despite all that had happened, he and Carol had found happiness, and were looking forward to having their first child. Stan knew that he must now face up to the responsibility of providing for, and protecting, his family. He did not want his child to have to endure the same hardships that he had faced. The economic Depression and the war had left so many Australians insecure and in desperate need. What Australia needed now was a larger population and an industrialised economy, and he was determined to do his bit to see that this happened.

He vowed to himself that his child would be given a roof over his or her head, clothes to wear, nourishing food, a good education and a stable family. *Australia must also look to its defence. We must never again allow our defence force to become as depleted as it had during the 1930s.* These thoughts were Stan's firm commitment to his family and his country.

If they had a boy, Stan would see that he grew up physically strong, mentally disciplined, and emotionally stable. At times this would require Stan to administer tough love. Not through physical abuse, but through his child's acceptance of the consequences of his actions, the development of a strong, independent character, and a determination of will to achieve those things in life his child would deem important.

Stan believed these things because his life's experience had taught him this was necessary for any child to meet the challenges of an unpredictable world, where an adult male's duty is to protect and provide for his family. He believed these things because he had needed these qualities to survive in the cruel, indifferent world he had navigated.

Stan accepted this as his responsibility, now that he was about to become a father, and he felt blessed for his good fortune and the love he and Carol shared. He also realised that his child would require love and emotional support if he or she was to mature into a well-rounded adult, but this Stan believed was more a task for Carol than for him. If the child was a girl, he was sure her mother would be able to guide her in what was necessary for a happy and successful life.

Stan took a deep breath, and his mind went back to the war years – the horror that he had gone through on the Kokoda Track, and the difficulties he and Carol had endured during the American presence in Brisbane. Then he remembered the kindness that Captain Levi had shown towards Jean and her baby, Lynda. Captain Levi had certainly come through for them, having gained American citizenship for Lynda and the insurance money left to her by her father. *Not all Americans are like Frank*, Stan thought.

Stan smiled when he remembered how that money had enabled Billy and Jean to buy their first home. Now they could provide everything that Lynda would ever need, something that Lynda's parents never had growing up. If only everyone could have a little to get them started in life like Billy and Jean. Perhaps then families could grow up much happier.

Stan reflected on America's war against Japan. He knew that the Americans had not been interested in a treaty with Australia until the Japanese had attacked Pearl Harbor. After that, things changed as America came to see Australia as a launching pad in their war against Japan. This approach had taken Japan's attention away from the American west coast, and made an invasion of Australia strategically important for the Japanese. Nevertheless, Stan had to admit that without America's assistance, Australia would surely have fallen into the hands of Japan. Put simply, Australia had been incapable of defending itself against the overwhelming might of the Imperial Japanese Army.

Stan had come to recognise that Americans and Australians shared common values, like a commitment to liberty and democracy and a rejection of tyranny. He could see how Australia and America could co-operate in the future to ensure the survival of these shared values. Australia would always be America's younger brother, but at least Australia could become a valued ally – a country that America could depend on to fight alongside them in resisting any tyrannical attack on liberty.

Carol moved up beside Stan and put her arm around his waist. Stan responded by putting his arm around her shoulders, and she snuggled in close to his chest. 'Penny for your thoughts,' she said.

'Nothing really, darling. Just admiring the view, and being grateful for everything we have.'

'Yes. We are fortunate.'

I am so happy that Carol seems to have overcome the

shock that Frank caused her, Stan thought. *I know she still has fretful nights when that incident in the Victory Café is relived in her mind, but she knows I am here for her, and that she can count on me.*

Carol wrapped her other arm around Stan and squeezed him tight. They had been through so much together. Even before the war they had supported each other, and now it seemed so natural that they should be together. Her mind went back to the years before the war. She remembered the argument between the government and the unions about selling pig iron to the Japanese after they had invaded Korea and China and were committing atrocities against the people of these countries. The unions called the then prime minister 'Pig Iron Bob', and had warned everyone that Australia would one day regret having helped the Japanese build their war machine.

It had been a very close thing for Australia, and had it not been for the Americans, and the great sacrifice our boys made on the Kokoda Track, we would surely have been invaded by Japan. She remembered the facts that had come out of the war trials held against the Japanese after the war, especially the cruel executions of Australian soldiers in the Lark and Gull forces, who had surrendered to the Japanese at Rabaul and Ambon.

Then there was the brutal treatment of Australian POWs who were ordered to build the Burma Railway – the beatings, the lack of food, little or no clothing, and inadequate shelter and medical supplies. *What was worse, however, was the treatment that the Japanese soldiers inflicted on the populations of the countries they conquered, particularly the women.* She shuddered to think what a Japanese occupation of Australia would have been like had the Japanese been victorious.

Since the war, there was a lot of talk about the small size of Australia's population. The catchcry now was 'populate or perish' and Carol took that cry to heart. She was determined to be a good wife and mother. She wanted at least four children, and she would be sure to provide a good home for all of them. Then her mind went back to her husband, and the deep love and commitment they had for each other. She wanted so much to help Stan in any way she could.

Poor Stan, Carol thought. *He still has nightmares about the Kokoda Track. He still has sleepless nights and cold sweats, but he is trying so hard to make a go of it, and I'll be here for him in any way I can. And now that we are having a child, I will devote myself to ensuring the stability of our family.*

THE END

AUTHOR'S OPINIONS ON AUSTRALIA'S SECURITY

JANUARY 2023

An examination of the historical detail surrounding the dispute between Curtin and Churchill over the return of Australian regular troops from Europe for the defence of their homeland clearly shows that not only did Churchill resist this development, but he also tried to divert the Australian convoy carrying the Australian troops back to Australia, and send them into Burma (now Myanmar). This abandonment of Australia's defence runs even deeper, however, because Churchill went further and convinced Roosevelt to give the 'European Conflict' priority over the 'Pacific Conflict'.[4] Clearly, none of this was done in Australia's interest, but it certainly was in Britain's interest.

As far as the American strategy for the Pacific conflict was concerned, President Roosevelt adopted

---

4 The First Washington Conference, code name ARCADIA, 22 December 1941 to 14 January 1942.

a brilliant plan. He would turn Australia into a huge American army base from which to launch his attack on the Imperial Japanese Army. (This was convenient for America because it took Japan's attention away from Hawaii and the West Coast of America, especially after the Battle of Midway fought in June of 1942). At the same time, he would rebuild the American navy and attack the Japanese out of Hawaii, thus splitting the Japanese line of advance and destroying their supply lines. In this way, he had the navy, led by Admiral Nimitz, and the army, led by General MacArthur, competing with each other over who was the more successful commander. A submarine base was also established at Fremantle, Western Australia, which attacked Japanese supply lines with such devastating effect.

Australians should be grateful for America's help in the defence of their homeland in their time of need, but they should also understand that that help aligned with America's strategy for the pursuit of its war in the Pacific. What can be indisputably concluded from this is that nations always pursue their foreign policy in terms of their own national self-interest. Australians should be clear minded about this when planning their own national defence. To do otherwise is folly.

Since the end of World War II, Australia has sought

to safeguard its national borders through the United Nations (UN). This has proven ineffective. Although every member nation of the UN agrees to guarantee the territorial integrity of all other member nations, history has shown us that this promise has been simply ignored, and the UN has been unable to stop conflicts from breaking out between its member nations. However, the UN has been effective in helping member nations in conflict with one another reach peace settlements to their conflict. This only occurs, though, when both sides to the conflict are actively searching for an end to hostilities.

Australia has also sought to safeguard its security through alliances and treaties. The most substantial of these is our ANZUS alliance with both America and New Zealand. To this end, Australia sought to encourage American investment in Australia, integrate our defence force with that of America's, and provide America with secret bases in Australia. Australia has also allowed an American marine base to be established in the Northern Territory and the American navy full access to all our ports, including submarine maintenance facilities in Western Australia. Furthermore, we have fought alongside the Americans in every conflict they have become involved in since the end of World War II.

We have even agreed to a non-nuclear pact with our

neighbouring nations, preferring instead to rely on the American nuclear umbrella for our security, and a belief that if Australia ever suffered a nuclear attack, America would retaliate on our behalf. Again, Australians need to accept the fact that America would do that only if it was in their national self-interest to do so. Keep in mind that Australia has been warned on two occasions that it could face a first strike nuclear attack by foreign powers. The first was from Russia in the 1980s (over the existence of American secret bases on Australian soil) and more recently by the Chinese (over Australia's criticism of the CCP).

It should also be noted that in the 1950s, Australia participated with Great Britain in the development of their nuclear bomb. Several bombs were tested on Australian soil, and in 1958, Australia opened its first nuclear reactor at Lucas Heights, a southern suburb of Sydney, which still operates today. So, the material and the technology were available for Australia to develop its own nuclear industry and deterrent, but Australia chose not to go down that path and instead go with the (cheaper) American nuclear umbrella strategy.

As can be seen, Australians have spent decades of blood and treasure, and endured threats from foreign powers trying to convince Americans that Australia is an ally upon which they can rely, and that the defence of Australia is in America's own national self-interest. All this has been done in the hope that if Australia's security was ever threatened, America would come to Australia's aid.

The ANZUS treaty signed by Australia, New Zealand and the United States has been a cornerstone of Australian foreign policy since the 1950s. Does the ANZUS alliance that Australia has entered into provide this security guarantee? The answer is yes and no. For example, what is it exactly that the ANZUS alliance guarantees Australia? Article IV of the treaty states:

> Each Party recognizes that an armed attack in the Pacific Area on any of the Parties would be dangerous to its own peace and safety and declares that it would act to meet the common danger in accordance with its *constitutional processes*.[5] (author's italics)

Australians need to understand that what this means is that if Australia is attacked, America agrees to send the issue to the American Congress for deliberation. The American president has the constitutional authority to make an emergency decision if this were to occur and send help, but the authority to declare war

---

5   http://www.austlii.edu.au/au/other/dfat/treaties/1952/2.html
     (accessed 07/11/2022)

rests solely with the American Congress and not the president. In the short term this can be advantageous for the country under attack. A good example of this is the president's and Congress's initial assistance to Vietnam, Afghanistan, Iraq, and its current material support of Ukraine. However, the longer a conflict continues, the more public support for the American commitment erodes, and with it, congressional resolution, as was the case with the Vietnam War (which I intend to examine in detail in my third book on the Vietnam War) and, in recent times, the wars in Iraq and Afghanistan.

Incidentally, America's and its allies' win/loss ratio since the end of World War II is abysmal. Korea was a draw, Vietnam was a loss, Iraq was a loss and Afghanistan was a loss. A draw and three losses. This hardly inspires confidence in America's strategy, and raises an important question: Are we witnessing a change in America's strategy? America is currently fighting a proxy war in Ukraine. That is, they supply Ukraine with the weapons and supplies they need to fight the war, but America and its allies do not engage. Also, the aid America and its allies supply to Ukraine is subject to endless discussions about what constitutes a defensive weapon and an offensive weapon. The reasoning behind this stems from the fear that America and its allies harbour about triggering a nuclear war. This is curious, since the communist countries harbour no such fear; at different times in the past, they have even threatened to launch a first strike nuclear attack against America and its allies.

And what of Taiwan? America's official position is one of strategic ambiguity. It appears Taiwan also will have to fight off an invasion on its own. Where does this leave Australia? Would America adopt a proxy war approach to Australia's defence? Clearly, Australia's position is somewhat different from that of either Ukraine or Taiwan because Australia has a treaty alliance with America. Nevertheless, Australians need to remember what the actual terms of that treaty are. America agrees to act in accordance with its constitutional process. What if Congress decides that it is not worth risking a nuclear war to fully defend Australia, as they have done with Ukraine, and possibly in the future, with Taiwan?

Incidentally, there was a defence treaty in existence during the Vietnam War (1962–1972). In 1954, the South-East Asian Treaty Organization (SEATO) was formed. It included the United States, France, Great Britain, New Zealand, Australia, the Philippines, Thailand and Pakistan. South Vietnam was an honouree member. SEATO was set up by America to act like a NATO pact for Asian nations, and its purpose was to prevent communism gaining ground in the region. This treaty did not, however, lead to a collective defence of South Vietnam, and was abandoned after the war. In 1967, the Association of South-East Asian Nations (ASEAN) was established. The founding countries were Indonesia, Malaysia, Philippines, Singapore and Thailand. The purpose of ASEAN was to promote political and economic cooperation, and regional stability. It was not, and today is not, a collective defence treaty. America and Australia were not invited to become members of ASEAN.

Another treaty that Australia has recently (2021) entered into is the AUKUS treaty. This treaty offers Australia an unprecedented opportunity because it allows Australia access to the latest, cutting-edge military technology available in both the United States and the United Kingdom. Nevertheless, this is only an opportunity. Australia must now be prepared to fund the acquisition and development of this technology.

Yet another cooperation between countries in the region is the QUAD, which is a strategic dialogue between Australia, India, Japan and the United States. It is not a defence treaty, but has led to unprecedented naval exercises involving all member countries. The major concern of the QUAD appears to be China's claims to the East and South China seas and its belligerent attitude in these areas. Also, India is concerned about the emerging presence of the Chinese navy in the Indian Ocean, and the new naval ports that China has acquired in Sri Lanka and Pakistan, which out-flank India and could be used to cut India's trading sea lanes. As well as this, India is anxious about its northern border with China, which periodically flares into open conflict.

As can be seen, all these treaties, alliances and dialogues are comforting, but all of them offer only limited security for Australia.

Unfortunately, Australia's reliance on America for its security has led to a number of problems for Australia's defence planners. Foremost among these is a lack of priority for defence funding in our federal budgets. Successive Australian governments have given top priority to social and corporate welfare spending, especially green corporate welfare, which has seen tens of billions of dollars already committed to future spending with more to come[6] and only secondary

---

6   Recent announcements include: $20B by the Australian federal government for an electricity grid upgrade (smh.com.au) and $47B for the green hydrogen project (energy.gov.au). Then there are the state government projects that are calling for federal assistance in funding. The most recent of these is the Queensland government's announcement of a $62B clean energy plan, which includes funding for a pumped hydro station and will be the largest in the world (abc.net.au). This highlights just three of many dozens of projects announced by Australian governments.

priority to defence funding. The current Australian Parliament has passed legislation pledging to cut carbon emissions by 43% by 2030 and to achieve net zero by 2050. These are highly ambitious targets, since no other country has come anywhere close to achieving such targets. This begs the following questions: How much public spending is Parliament willing to sacrifice to achieve these targets? Will a limit (as a % of GDP) be placed on this highly ambitious public project, or will it be achieved at any cost? Since the government is also committed (at some time in the future) to balancing future federal budgets and even producing surplus budgets in order to pay down our huge national debt, which current areas of government spending will be sacrificed to achieve these targets? With the American economy in recession, Europe's uncertain future following its energy crisis, and the OECD downgrading Australia's economic growth from 2.5 to 2% for next year,[7] the Australian government will struggle to keep all these commitments.

This is not to say that social and corporate welfare spending is not important, or even that it should be given a low priority. Of course, social and corporate welfare is important to any wealthy, civilised nation, and should enjoy a high priority. The question that must be

---

7   OECD, June 2022 forecasts.

addressed, however, is whether it is prudent to gain one at the expense of the other. Is it wise to increase spending on social or corporate welfare if it means reducing funding for Australia's security? Perhaps an answer can be found in ensuring equal priority for both. That is, don't achieve one at the expense of the other. Don't cut defence funding in order to achieve some new social welfare ambition or some new corporate welfare initiative, as has been the case in Australia's past budget planning.

This leads to yet another question. What would be an appropriate level of funding for Australia's defence? Obviously, Australia's level of funding was inadequate prior to the outbreak of hostilities in World War II, and Australians rightly condemned their politicians for allowing Australia to be put in such a vulnerable position.

Where should one look for guidance in this area? NATO makes member nations pledge to spend a minimum of 2% of their GDP on defence. It is true that some member nations reneged on this promise. Chief among these was Angela Merkel, ex-Chancellor of Germany, who, since the Russian invasion of Ukraine, stands condemned by the current chancellor, Olaf Scholz, and the German people, for having allowed Germany's defence force, the Bundeswehr, to be so wilfully depleted. In response to this neglect, Olaf Scholz has decided to make Germany the third-largest military spender in the world, and in the future, Germany will have the largest land army in Europe. This is an emergency measure that puts a heavy burden on the German budget, and is the exact opposite of what Angela Merkel's approach was, which had viewed Putin as no threat to European security. A good starting point for Australia, therefore, would be to learn from Germany's mistake.

Would an appropriate level of funding for Australia's defence, then, be 2% of GDP during peacetime? Perhaps, perhaps not. As early as 1987, Professor Dibbs produced a white paper on Australia's defence and found that an appropriate level of spending would be in the order of 2.6% to 3% of GDP. Where then to draw the line? Whatever the decision, should this amount be increased in a time when tensions arise between Australia and a potential enemy, especially if that potential enemy begins to develop territorial ambitions in Australia's region?

Finally, it should be indisputably accepted by all that if Australia is ever again threatened with invasion and occupation, the only reasonable response would be to give defence funding top priority, and commit all available resources and human power to the defence of Australia, as was the case in Australia's past.

In December 1941, John Curtin delivered these words to the Australian people, informing them of the coming sacrifice they would have to make:

> Australians must realise that to place the nation on a wartime footing, every citizen must place himself, his private and business affairs, his entire mode of living, on a war footing. The civilian way of life cannot be any less rigorous, can contribute no less than that which the fighting men have to follow.
>
> I demand that Australians everywhere realise that Australia is now inside the firing lines.[8]

Do Australians really want to allow a situation to arise where an Australian prime minister feels it necessary to deliver a speech containing such dire warnings and demands? How can such a situation be avoided in future?

A big benefit for Australia, if it were to adopt the minimum 2.6%–3% model for defence funding, would be the deterrence it would provide. That is, it would be less likely that Australia would find itself in a position

---

8   *The Task Ahead* speech by Prime Minister John Curtin first published by The Herald (Melbourne), 27 December 1941.

where it had to adopt the third stage of committing all available resources to meet the challenge of invasion and occupation, simply because any potential aggressor would know that it would have to pay a very high price indeed to achieve its military ambitions. Surely, this should be the goal of Australia's defence policy? To take action intended to avoid open hostilities.

Unfortunately for Australia, however, the funding for Australia's security has been sadly neglected for decades. As was pointed out earlier, in Professor Dibbs' 1987 Defence White Paper, Professor Dibbs warned the then Australian government led by Bob Hawke against their band-aid approach to Australia's defence, and pointed out that what was needed was to spend in the range of 2.6% to 3% of GDP. Although the Hawke government did increase its Defence budget, it never reached the required level suggested by Professor Dibbs, whose warning was largely ignored, and in later years most politicians turned their attention towards the threat from terrorism, but this was never seen as an existential threat, and was handled adequately with low budget spending. Consequently, Australian politicians have continuously allowed defence funding to fall below a 2% of GDP level, which has resulted in Australia's defence planners now finding themselves in a perilous position.

Combining this with problems arising from our procurement program, enlistment levels and strategic reserve levels, means that Australia will need to raise its defence funding to a level beyond the 3%, especially now that Australia is faced with a potential aggressor. Defence planners have advised their politicians that Australia faces a possibility of war in the near future,[9] and that our defence forces are understaffed and lacking the necessary military arsenal to face such a challenge. This is a high level, existential threat, and will need much greater budget sacrifice than Australians have experienced in recent times.

Owing to the availability of new defence technology, the Australian government has been advised by its defence planners that Australia needs to replace its current Collins Class diesel submarines with eight nuclear-powered submarines in order to prepare for the challenges ahead, but the current government planning is to deliver them in twenty years when the potential for war is very near. What then, is to be done?

Senator Jim Molan (AO DSC) addresses this question in his latest book: *Danger on Our Doorstep*. I will not repeat all the excellent arguments that Senator Molan makes, encouraging Australians to establish a

---

9   Jim Molan, *Danger on Our Doorstep*, HarperCollins Publishers Australia
     Pty Limited, Sydney, NSW 2000, p.31.

national strategy[10] to meet the very real current threat to our national security, but rather briefly highlight some of the more obvious shortfalls in our current defence preparedness. Please note these are shortfalls, so I am not recommending that they all have to be addressed immediately or even concurrently, but rather that they will need to be addressed in the near future and that a national strategy seems like a good point to start so as to determine what the proper priorities should be.

Obviously, Australia will need to request special consideration for its urgent needs from the Americans. What is in Australia's best interest is to have delivery of the Virginia-class submarines as early as possible. This will mean that Australia does whatever is necessary to have these submarines in the hands of the RAN quickly, and if that means leasing them from the American navy or buying the submarines from American shipbuilders then that is what must be done. Australia will also need to train Australian submariners in the use of these new weapons, and maintenance facilities will also need to be built and maintenance staff trained. The argument that Australia does not currently possess the maintenance facilities for nuclear submarines and so should not take early delivery of them can be overcome by simply

10   Ibid., 149.

having them maintained at an American facility until an Australian facility is developed.

If Australia is to build nuclear submarines in the future, it will be necessary for the shipbuilders here to start immediately to train their staff in designing the submarines, develop the skills of the shipbuilders themselves, and build the necessary shipbuilding facilities. What can be seen from all this is that the Australian government must start immediately on these projects, and talk of acquiring them in twenty years is unrealistic planning for the threat Australia now faces.

These nuclear submarines also need larger crews than our current Collins Class submarines, which the navy already has trouble crewing. Australia will have to offer greater incentives for their submariners in the future, if the nuclear submarines are to be properly crewed. Australia is also experiencing trouble with the Hunter-class frigate which will replace the existing Anzac-class frigates. These problems will have to be overcome, which will once again raise the funding level for the acquirement of these ships.

Overcoming these problems will drive the funding level for Australia's defence to at least 2.6% up to 3% of GDP mentioned by Professor Dibbs. But there is more to consider. What the war in Ukraine has shown is the importance of missile, drone and precision-targeting artillery technology to modern warfare. Therefore, if Australia is to be prepared to face the potential threat to its security that its defence planners say is likely, then it will be necessary to acquire the ability to manufacture these items in Australia. This will mean an expansion of Australia's defence industry. All this is necessary before even considering problems like the shortfalls in Australia's strategic oil reserves and Australia's military arsenal. There is also the question of the size of the ADF itself, which will need to at least double, both in regular and reserve personnel – not to mention the emergence of new technologies like laser-defence weapons, uncrewed submarines and hypersonic missiles.

With Australia's current security position under threat, the unprepared state of its defence force, and the new opportunity afforded Australia under the AUKUS Treaty, it should be self-evident that the appropriate level for present-day defence funding should go beyond the 3% of GDP level as mentioned before. It is true that such a level of spending on defence will require sacrifice and determination on the part of Australians and their government. On the other hand, once Australia has reached an adequate level of preparedness, there is no reason why funding could not return to the 2.6% to 3% levels.

On 24 October 2022, the federal government announced in its Mini Budget that it would increase defence spending by 7.4% on the 2021–22 Budget. Allowing for inflation, this represents a net increase of 3.8%. Although it is encouraging to know that the federal government recognises the importance of defence spending at this time, this still only represents 1.98% of Australia's current GDP.[11] Remember that Professor Dibbs made his recommendations based on there being no visible threat to Australia's security, whereas Australia's position today has changed to that of an imminent, visible threat.

Given all this, is it necessary to point out that the priority given to the level of funding for Australia's security since the end of World War II has been inadequate? One consequence of this lack of priority is that Australia today finds itself in a similar position to that of the 1930s when Australia depended on the British Empire for its security. I hope that *Kokoda Mist* has clearly highlighted the foolishness of such a defence policy. The only difference today is that our dependence is now on American military might, which

11 Australian Strategic Policy Institute (aspistrategist.org.au), (accessed 25/10/2022), p.1.

is no longer what it once was, as was the case with the British forces in the late 1930s.

With the drums of war beating in Europe and the bugles of war being heard across the Pacific, where does that leave Australia? What if America finds itself fighting a war on two fronts as it did in World War II? Would the European Theatre once again be given top priority over the Pacific? If placed in such a position, would America allow Australia access to the military hardware it would need to defend itself? Would America even have the capacity to accommodate such a request?

With these considerations in mind, would it not be prudent for Australia to adopt a more self-reliant approach in its defence planning, and fund its security accordingly? Such an approach would not only act as a deterrent against a potential enemy, but would also demonstrate to our alliance partners that we are serious about our partnership and willing to make the necessary sacrifices to strengthen the alliance.

www.ingramcontent.com/pod-product-compliance
Lightning Source LLC
Chambersburg PA
CBHW030748190726
48285CB00003B/749